THE GUPPY PRINCE

THE SILVER ISLES: BOOK ONE

C.W. GRAY

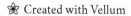

*D*over Rees floated in the deepest part of his creek, enjoying the rushing sound of the waterfall to his right. Sunlight filtered through the water, glinting off the deep blue of his guppy tail. His thin and delicate caudal fin spread out like an elegant fan, dancing through the warm water as he swayed.

His favorite smooth and colorful pebbles were strewn around below him, and he admired the shells he had collected and placed beside them. Dover breathed deeply and enjoyed the peace and quiet. No one mocked him or bossed him around. No one watched him with cold eyes and hidden smirks. *I wish I could stay here forever.*

Sudden movement beside him jarred him from his thoughts and he laughed when Chubber grabbed a bright pink stone in his small brown paws and swam away. Dover's otter friend liked to steal Dover's shinies then share them with him again later.

A brook trout swam past him and Dover debated grabbing it for an early lunch, but he wasn't too hungry yet. Lately, he'd been eating less and less, and he couldn't make himself care.

The quiet water around him hummed as Nami quickly swam to him. His best friend's guppy tail was a lovely pink pattern with black dots, and her short black hair floated around her head. The cat with a mermaid tail on her black tankini top made him smile. He loved her purr-maid shirts.

"Have you eaten today, Your Highness?" she asked.

Dover scowled. "Don't call me that."

"When you're acting like a pouting asswipe, that's what you get called." Nami wrapped her arms around him and settled her head on his shoulder. "What's wrong with you, Dover?"

Dover had no answer for her. All he knew was he felt empty inside and it was harder and harder to get up in the morning. "I think I ate some bad clams."

"Every day for the past two months?" Nami leaned back and glared at him, her dark eyes seeing right through him.

Chubber came to his rescue, swimming in between them and wrapping his lean body across Dover's shoulders. "Chubber wants to get a snack."

Nami sighed, bubbles filling the water around her. "Mom is in your cottage making lunch. You're worrying us, bluetail."

Dover stroked a hand through her hair, then shoved her down and pushed up, swimming toward the surface.

"Damn it!" Nami swam after him.

He laughed, heart warming. *Someone cares about me.* It wasn't his family, but Nami and her mom were closer to him than his parents or any of his twelve siblings.

Chubber clung to his back and nibbled on his ear until he mentally apologized. Chubber cared about him the most.

His creek was deep, but it didn't take him long to reach the surface. Shauna waited for them on the shore, hands on her hips. Chubber's mother, Shell, stood on her hind legs beside the mermaid, chirping loudly. Uh oh. He really was in trouble.

"You didn't eat breakfast, did you?" The wind blew strands of Shauna's pink hair across her face, ruining her glare.

"Sorry, Shauna."

She sighed. "I made your favorite."

"Grilled shrimp salad?" Dover's stomach rumbled.

"With avocado, papaya, mango, and pineapple. All your favorites." Shauna gave him a soft look. "Come eat, bluetail."

Dover summoned his human legs and a few seconds later, walked out of the creek, naked, with Chubber clinging to his shoulder. Shauna handed him a deep teal sarong, and he tied it about his waist.

Shell crawled up his leg and into his arms, then rubbed her slick furry face against his. She was a bit heavier than Chubber, but he was still a baby.

"Why does he get all the loving?" Nami asked, grumbling as she tied a sarong around her own waist.

Dover chuckled when Shauna arched an eyebrow at her daughter. "Did you say something, sweetness?"

"No, ma'am," Nami said, wincing.

"You two come eat lunch." Shauna turned around and walked toward Dover's large cottage.

Dover closed his eyes for a moment and savored the feel of the moss-covered rocks under his feet, and the comfortable breeze quickly drying his curly blue hair. He loved his home so much. It was his sanctuary.

"Do you need a moment to commune with nature and shit?" Nami shoved him from behind, making him laugh.

"Maybe I do." A gleam of metal caught his eye and Dover bent to pick up the ten-strand, graduated freshwater-pearl necklace someone had left on a large rock near his creek. The clasp was a diamond-encrusted, silver guppy tail. "Look. Another necklace."

Nami made a face. "Why doesn't someone leave expensive jewelry on a rock for me?"

"It's always guppy themed," he said, smiling softly and stroking the pearls. He'd been getting the gifts for years now. He suspected it was one of his brothers raiding the royal treasure vault. *Maybe Kai or Kit want me to look the part of a prince.*

Nami took the necklace and fastened it around his neck, dodging Chubber and Shell to hook the clasp. "At least this fancy thing makes you smile."

Dover sighed and walked up the worn path toward his cottage, admiring the thick trees and colorful flowers as Shell rubbed her head against his chin. "I don't want to move to the castle."

"What?" Nami gave him a horrified look. "Why would you do that?"

"Father says I have to move to the castle with the others by the end of the month. Lord Eades told him it was time I married and started popping out babies."

Dover stopped in front of his home, admiring the two story, stone cottage. Lilies, lace leaf, and hibiscus flowers lined the front flowerbeds, and colorful mandevilla vines climbed the posts on either sides of the steps leading to the covered porch. Wind chimes chinked a peaceful tune as they shook in the gentle breeze.

"This is my home," he said, even though he knew something was missing from his cozy sanctuary.

"Lord Eades wouldn't try that shit with your alpha siblings," Nami said, voice angry. "They can't make you move to the castle and get married, can they? I hate swimming in the ocean and I can't *not* see you every day."

Shauna stood in the doorway. "What's this? Why would you leave, Dover?"

Dover shrugged and explained his father's request. "I don't want to leave, but Father *is* the king."

Shauna was quiet as she set plates on the old, scratched wooden table. "Sit down and eat, bluetail."

Shell rubbed his face one more time, then skittered out the door. She had young pups to care for back in the old beaver dam she called home.

Chubber muttered into Dover's hair, then jumped from his shoulder and ran to his nest in the corner of the living room. He put the brightly colored stone with all the others beside his bed.

The living room, kitchen, and dining room were all open spaces filled with sunlight from the large windows. Colorful pieces of glass hung from the ceiling, and his favorite shinies were scattered around the room. Soft pillows covered the furniture, and a small stone fountain sat in the corner close to the stairs, water flowing constantly. *This is home. How can I possibly leave it?*

The castle was pure opulence, but was so cold. He would have to wear his prince mask every single day and would have very little peace from the stupid, judgmental nobility.

"Dover? I said sit." Shauna rubbed his shoulder. "You haven't been eating right."

Dover did as he was told and dug into the tasty shrimp salad. Shauna was the best cook and had taught him several of her recipes. He was good, but Shauna was the best and the pompous castle chef could suck a shark dick.

Nami scowled at the table, even as she ate her own lunch. "When did the King tell you?"

"Yesterday."

"That doesn't explain your mopey behavior for the past couple of months," Shauna said, passing him a bowl of crusty homemade bread.

Dover shrugged. "I don't know what's wrong." He looked up from his plate. "I went swimming last week and ended up three miles past the trench. I don't even remember leaving my creek and I had to have swum down the river, into the ocean, past the reefs and Latch Bay, and over the trench. I've never swam that far before."

Shauna looked worried. "That's dangerous, Dover. You're not a warrior and there are a lot of predators in the open sea. A guppy tail like you would make a shark a good meal."

"That's if the Coalswells don't get you." Nami shook her head. "Why would you do that? How could that even happen? The borders are well guarded. Why would any of the sentries let a prince past them?"

"The guards don't see me," Dover said, bitterly. "I'm just another guppy tail. I *wish* I was just a guppy tail and Shauna were my mom and you were my sister."

Shauna made an odd croaking sound. "I love you, bluetail. I wish you were mine too."

"I keep wanting to swim out," Dover said quietly. "I don't understand it, but it's like something is calling me."

Shauna gasped, eyes widening. "The mating call. It's the mating call."

Dover blinked, mouth dropping open. He had a mate? Someone meant just for him. Someone who would accept him as he was. How could it be possible?

Nami made a face. "Seriously? Where is it calling him? The Silver Isles go north and south, not west."

The Silver Isles were a long strip of islands in the middle of the Atlantic Ocean. They stretched for over two thousand miles, right along the Mid-Atlantic

Ridge. Latch Bay was the most Southern city on the Isles and the capital of the Southern Silver Isles.

Shauna rolled her eyes. "There are merfolk all over the world, sweetness." She tapped her chin. "West of Latch Bay is open ocean though. No mer would want to live there. The closest colony is near… the Virgin Islands, maybe? I'm not sure. What exact direction are you being pulled?"

Dover closed his eyes and let the pull take over. Time seemed to stand still, until his back hit the hardwood floor, making his eyes pop open. Nami sat on him. "What the hell?"

"You got up and went for the door," she said. "Your face was all stupid looking."

"Nami, get off of the poor boy." Shauna knelt beside him. "What direction, bluetail?"

"Northwest." He pushed Nami away and laughed when she tickled his side. "Stop it, polka dots."

Shauna gave him a concerned look. "North America. You were going toward North America."

"You can't possibly swim all the way there to find your mate," Nami said.

Dover lay back on the ground, smiling dreamily. "My mate."

Chubber's whiskered face appeared above him and the otter squeaked at him. Of course, Chubber would go with him. That meant he couldn't swim across the ocean.

"What can I do?"

Shauna gave him a thoughtful look. "Give me a day. I'll figure it out."

～

LATER THAT AFTERNOON, Dover dropped his sarong on the beach and waded into the ocean before summoning his tail.

"All hail the guppy prince," Lorelei said, voice full of derision.

Thanks, sister dear. Dover should have known better than to try swimming where his other siblings could see him. He only really got along with Kit and Kai. The others either ignored or mocked him, especially when they were surrounded by other merfolk from the Silver Isles nobility.

Dover's sister sat with her friends on their favorite grouping of rocks along the shallows of the royal beach. Her bright blonde hair and the deep orange and electric-blue of her angelfish tail stood out among most of the other mermaids. Her large breasts were barely covered in her bikini top and many of the aristocratic merfolk on the beach watched her with hunger in their eyes.

"Go back to the freshwater, guppy prince," his sister, Eugenia said. She looked bored as she floated in the water, her pink and blue parrotfish tail gleaming in the sun.

The merman at her side laughed, eyes smirking. "Guppies don't belong in the ocean, royal or not."

Dover swam deeper into the water, ignoring the insults. Most guppy tails stayed in one of the large rivers or the many lakes further inland, and he couldn't really blame them. It's what he preferred too.

"Look at his tail," the merman said, voice carrying in the water. "It's so... plebian. Are you sure he's your brother, Eugenia?"

Dover left them behind before he could hear his sister's reply. If Kai had been there, no one would have dared say anything about Dover's tail. His eldest brother was stern and distant, but he was also very protective of his family.

I love my tail, Dover thought, heart sore. He thought Shauna and Nami were the most beautiful mers in all the ocean. Forget the angel tails and parrotfish tails. They were nothing compared to his friends.

The real problem was that a good portion of the castle servants were guppy tails which made Dover a bit of an eyesore in the royal court. All of the noble families had a more exotic heritage that *showed distinction and good breeding*. At least that was what Lord Eades said. Guppy tails lived all over the world and were the most common merfolk.

Rumor had it his great-grandmother on his mother's side had an affair with one of her servants. Dover supposed he was proof enough to make it more than a rumor.

He tried to push the nonsense away and enjoy his swim since he didn't visit the beach often. His own sanctuary usually kept him plenty happy. The restlessness hit him hard once Nami and Shauna left. Chubber was taking a nap, so Dover decided to go for a swim.

He swam over the royal coral gardens and spotted his brother, Kit, playing with his daughter, Pearl. The two had matching clownfish tails and fiery-red hair. They zipped around the corals, playing hide and seek.

Dover got on well with Kit, but his older brother lived in the castle and had Pearl to take care of, so they didn't get to spend a lot of time together.

He grinned as he watched Pearl grab her daddy's tail and squeal. Kit laughed, then looped his tail up and grabbed her, hugging the toddler tight.

Dover sighed. Their parents would never have done such a thing. The King and Queen of the Southern Silver Isles had certain expectations to meet and playing with their children was not one of them.

Dover swam by without saying hello. He didn't feel much like playing, though he knew his brother would welcome him.

He quickly reached the Latch Bay Reefs and couldn't help but admire the beauty of the sea life around him. Merfolk kept the oceans clean and healthy, though the land-dwellers hardly thanked them.

A herd of hippocampi swam above him, so Dover moved closer to the reefs. The powerful animals were protected in the Silver Isles, so they were a common sight. The deep green, blue, and purple water horses were one of the many things that drew the tourists.

Several guppy-tailed workers swam around, completing their afternoon checkup of the coral reefs and wildlife. Dover waved to his friend Moore. The merman was in charge of tending the reefs that surrounded Latch Bay.

After the herd passed, Dover left the reefs behind.

Traffic started to pick up as he reached the first small trench surrounding the city. Warriors patrolled the trench, ever watchful for trouble, though they paid him no attention.

Dover stopped and floated as he watched the bustling underwater city of Latch Bay in the distance. The city had an uppercity on the island and an undercity that lay beneath the surface of the bay. Merfolk needed both land and water to fulfill all their needs, and Latch Bay was the perfect balance of both.

A small underwater tour bus moved past him, reminding Dover that the two parts of the city were full of locals and visitors both. Dover hated the crowds and all the noise, even though it was nice to see different species. Inland there were only merfolk and a few aquatic shifters. There were no humans, vampires, witches, or any other of the hundreds of species that lived in the world.

A stingray-tailed merman bumped into him, scowling before moving on, reminding Dover not to linger in the growing crowd outside the city. He watched the man's winged tail glide through the water before moving on.

He swam toward his father's home. The large castle in the center of the city was made of shining white stone and thick, clear glass. The underwater portion was surrounded by seagrass and colorful corals while the land portion had exquisite landscaped gardens.

Dover gave the beautiful structure a wary look before swimming through one of the servant entrances. Time to check up on the family. Unfortunately. Maybe Shauna and Nami would be wrong, and his father would be happy that Dover had heard the mating call.

CHAPTER 2

*B*en Elliott sent another full rack of dishes through the industrial dishwasher. The restaurant he worked in wasn't big, but it got a lot of business from tourists in the summer. He pulled a stack of plates a server had dropped off over and cleaned them before starting to fill a new rack.

"Fuck, my feet hurt," Stewart told Ryan. The two servers unloaded trays full of dishes.

"Welcome to tourist season at the beach," Ryan said, laughing. "If you're still around in the winter, you'll get a break. Trust me."

"Why aren't you limping?" Stewart asked. "You worked a double tonight."

Ryan's grin was pure predator. "Wolf shifter, remember? I'm bigger and badder than you puny humans."

Stewart snorted and looked at Ben. "Did he or did he not scream when he saw that spider next to the dumpster yesterday and come get you to kill it?"

Ben grunted, but gave Ryan a sympathetic look. The young shifter didn't like spiders. Lots of people didn't.

Ryan sniffed. "I don't know what you're talking about." He turned and left.

Stewart laughed. "Should I tell him that you just moved it to the tree line?"

Ben grinned. "Maybe not."

Stewart cackled as he left the dishwashing station.

The next hour moved quickly as the last of the customers left and the kitchen closed down. The servers finished their side work and cashed in their tips while the cooks did the prep for the next morning.

Ben finished the dishes, put them up, and sanitized his station before taking out the last of the garbage. He stood under the street light beside the dumpster and rolled his stiff shoulders. His job wasn't too bad. He had plenty of time to think and most people didn't mind that he was quiet.

His eye caught on the thin web clinging to one of the nooks of the dumpster. "Miss Spider, you really shouldn't make this your home. Ryan's screeching hurts the ears, and they pick up the trash every morning."

He grabbed a piece of cardboard from one of the broken boxes and gently slid the big, fat spider onto it before walking to the tree line. He went farther this time, hoping the spider would find a good home.

Rustling in a bush startled him and he froze in place. A big, grey wolf walked slowly out of the bush, a knapsack dangling in its mouth. Ryan's golden wolf eyes gave Ben a look of betrayal when he saw the spider.

"It's just a little spider," Ben reminded the wolf shifter. "You're a big badass, remember?"

Ryan growled around his package and turned around, leaving Ben and the spider behind.

"See what I mean, Miss Spider? You really need to make your home in one of these trees or Ryan may get up the courage to squash you." Ben gently helped the spider to the closest tree, then turned around.

He yelped at the sudden appearance of the short figure in front of him.

Old Hester smiled, chuckling. "I love scaring you young'uns. Come on handsome, you act like you never seen an old lady before."

Ben cleared his throat. "Hi Hester. You startled me." The old witch was well known in the small coastal town. She sold charms to the tourists and read cards for the locals. She lived in one of the ramshackle beach houses that lined the coast, more specifically, in the one next to his own.

"I need a ride home, Benny." She grinned, her teeth crooked, but her eyes warm and friendly.

"Yes, ma'am." He knew better than to point out he rode a bike and she had rheumatoid arthritis. She liked the wind in her wiry grey hair and he wouldn't begrudge her a thing like that.

He walked with her back to the restaurant and made sure the doors were locked and the security on. He handed her his extra helmet. He'd taken to carrying it with him for just this occasion. The old woman had a way of finding him, no matter where he was.

He got on and helped her load onto the seat behind him before pushing off. He smiled when Hester wrapped her arms around his waist and leaned her head against his back. He liked the witch.

Ben pulled off the highway and started down the winding beach road. He enjoyed the quiet night and the fresh air. He had grown up in Georgia, but had loved visiting his great-aunt during the summer.

Aunt Prue had lived in Burnsley, South Carolina her whole life, and when she'd died, she'd left him her house. He had decided not to reenlist, so the timing had been perfect, even though he missed her. She had been a kindhearted woman and had taught him a lot of things that his parents never bothered with.

He pulled into the graveled drive of Hester's beach house. She slipped off his bike and took off the helmet and patted his cheek. "Thanks for the ride, handsome. When you get ready to sell your house, talk to Ryan. The boy is looking for his own place and he could use a break."

Ben frowned. "I'm not planning on selling."

Hester laughed and handed him the helmet. "You will." She gave him a soft look. "You're a gentle soul, Ben, but you're a fighter too. Don't hesitate to fight for what's yours."

He watched her, puzzled, as she made her way to the door. Her familiar, a large grey and white cat, watched him from the window, green eyes calm and knowing. Giving up on understanding the woman, he turned around and drove the short distance to his own house.

Aunt Prue's house had been worn and in need of a good coat of paint when he'd inherited it. After a year of living there, Ben had managed to fix it up. The small two-bedroom house was right on the beach and had a nice deck on the back. There was even a dock a mile down the road where he stored his fishing boat. *Why would I sell it?*

A brown furry face filled the front window and barked at him.

"Coming, buddy." Ben parked his bike and hurried to unlock the front door.

Otis almost knocked him over as he ran out to the front yard to do his business. Ben winced. It had been a long shift.

His dog was a golden doodle with curly brown fur. The same day he had left Fort Benning in Georgia, he had headed toward South Carolina with nothing but an old beat-up truck, his bike, and a couple of duffel bags. He had found Otis at a truck stop. The puppy had been starving, filthy, and covered in fleas.

Otis finished his business and ran to Ben, woofing softly.

Ben knelt and hugged him. "I'm sorry you had to wait, Otis. Another few long days and I'll have some time off. We can go fishing."

Otis licked his face and Ben laughed. "You just like the snacks I bring when we go fishing."

After feeding Otis and fixing a quick dinner for himself, Ben stretched out in the lounge chair on the back deck. The clear night sky was full of stars and the crash of the waves on the shore soothed him.

Otis climbed into his lap, the big dog moving around until he was comfortable with his head settled on Ben's chest. "Why would I sell this place, Otis? It's paid for and quiet. I like my job well enough, and I have you."

"Woof."

"Yeah, I love you too, buddy." Ben smoothed a hand over his dark, toffee-colored hair. He was still getting used to having more than stubble, and the thick and springy curls were getting a little out of control. He thought about calling Eloise, but she had an early shift tomorrow and it was late.

Otis leaned up and licked his chin.

"I'm not lonely, Otis. I'm really not."

Otis' brown eyes were knowing as they watched him.

"I have a good life." Ben leaned his head back and looked at the stars. "Maybe having an omega of my own would be good. Stewart and Jennifer seem happy together."

Otis' tongue hung out of his mouth as he grinned.

"My omega would have to be a man." Ben swallowed hard. "Mom and Dad won't like that."

The day he'd come out to them was the last day they had bothered to talk to him at all. He had been about to enlist in the Marine Corps and had gathered every bit of courage he had to tell them. They had reacted exactly as expected.

"Woof."

"You're right. They don't matter anyway. No one here cares that I'm gay. Remember when Stewart made me and Ryan go on a date?" Ben laughed. "That was horrible. I can't believe Hester cut in and ate dinner with us before walking me home. Ryan thought that was the funniest shit he'd ever seen."

Ben thought it had happened exactly how it should have. He and Ryan made good friends, but he didn't think they would have suited as lovers.

"Let's get some rest, Otis." Ben maneuvered the two of them out of the chair.

After a quick shower, he let Otis out one more time, then the two climbed into bed. The house was quiet, but the wind and waves were some comfort. *An omega would be nice, but why would I sell this place?*

"BRING OTIS WITH YOU," Stewart called out, tossing his apron into the backseat of his car. "You know Jenn loves your dog."

"Otis is a good boy," Ryan said, yawning. "Why are we having a cook-out at one in the morning?"

"Because we're hungry and we work late," Stewart said. "Jenn already invited everyone, so I think it's turning into a party."

Ben grunted. He would much rather work on a new project or go to bed early. *I'm too old for a party.*

The three men jumped when Hester appeared next to them. "Where the hell did you come from, Hester?" Ryan asked, hand pressed to his chest.

"None of your business." Hester scowled. "I need a ride to the party, Ben. We can take your truck so Otis can come."

Ryan laughed and patted his back. "Don't you feel loved?"

Ben sighed. It looked like he had to go now. "I'll pick you up."

Hester grinned. "I need a ride home now too."

Of course you do, he thought.

Forty-five minutes later, Ben parked his truck on the side of Stewart and Jenn's street. There were already several vehicles there. "Ready, Hester?"

The old woman looked at him, eyes hard. "There better be no foolin' around Benny. You hear me?"

Ben blinked. "What?"

Hester patted his cheek. "You need to save yourself for your mate?"

Ben opened his mouth, then closed it. *What the hell?*

"Next week is gonna be a real good week, Ben. Get the beer from the back, okay?"

Ben did as he was told and gave a manly squeak when he came face to face with a beaver. "Damn it, Eloise!"

The beaver's form shimmered for a moment, then elongated and morphed into a young woman with dark brown hair. Between her love of pranks and crude beaver jokes, Eloise was the town menace. Unfortunately, she was also his best friend.

Eloise fell against the two cases of beer, laughing. "You should have seen your face, Ben. Oh, dam, that was so much fun. Get it? Dam?" She laughed harder.

Hester cackled. "It's not nice to startle the poor humans, girly. Now, put your clothes on. You got a little longer than Ben, but you don't need to be showing off the goods either."

Eloise scowled and stood up, posing for them. "Whatcha talking about, old woman? These goods are too impressive to hide."

Ben rolled his eyes and grabbed the beer before leaving the two laughing women behind. He met Ryan at the door and the two took a couple of the beers to Stewart's back porch. Stewart and Jen didn't live on the beach, but they had a nice view of a wooded area.

Ryan stretched out in a chair and yawned. "It was busy tonight."

"Make good money?"

The wolf grinned. "Yeah. The tourists always get generous when they get tipsy."

Ben thought about what Hester had said. "You doing alright at the pack house?"

Ryan made a face. "I keep annoying Dahlia. Her mate's pregnant and she's especially grumpy since she's worried about Alicia." He looked wistful for a moment. "I'd like my own place one day. Maybe somewhere on the beach."

Ben grunted and handed the shifter another beer. "Hester helped them, right?" Dahlia was the alpha of the local wolf pack. She and Alicia had struggled for years to conceive. They were an alpha and beta pairing, so fertility had been a problem.

Ryan took a long drink. "Yeah. It took some time, but it worked. I'm really happy for them, don't get me wrong. I'm just afraid I'll mess something up for them. I'm too old to be living in the pack house anyway, even if I'm the alpha's little brother."

Ben grunted again. *What's Hester scheming?*

"Benny," Eloise said and sat in his lap. "Why won't Hester let me flirt with Jolene?"

Ryan laughed. "Maybe she's had a premonition about something bad happening if you mess around with Jolene."

"She told Ben to keep his pants on too." Eloise sniffed and settled her head on his shoulder. "She's so rude."

Ryan grinned. "Witches know stuff, Ellie. Ben is practically virginal anyway. Trust me. We see each other almost every day, so I would have smelled it on him if he had been with anyone the past year."

Ben scowled. "You don't know what you're talking about." Okay. Maybe the wolf *did* know what he was talking about. It had been a while.

"Good point," Eloise said. "He'd smell all sexed up, even after a few showers."

Sometimes it sucked to be human.

CHAPTER 3

$\mathcal{D}$over swam through the busy halls of the castle, trying to stay out of the way of the guppy-tailed servants. They smiled at him as they swam past and Dover felt his nervousness start to drain away.

"Your Highness, why are you in the servants' hall?" Ervin's hand on Dover's shoulder made him pause. The green guppy-tailed merman was the castle's Steward and had always been kind to Dover. There had been more than one time the merman had held him as he cried after Lorelai had said something particularly cruel.

Dover bit his lip. "Do you know if Father has a moment?"

Ervin gave him a gentle smile. "Let's go check, shall we? His assistant mentioned he had a busy schedule today, but I'm sure he would like to see you."

Dover followed him through the water-filled hallways. The servants' entrance was plain solid walls and lighting, and he knew they had left it behind when the plain lighting turned to fancy strands of fairy lights that glinted off the jewel-encrusted murals decorating the walls. Sand, shells, coral, and sea urchins covered the floor, adding to the beauty of the royal castle.

"How have you been, Prince Dover?" Ervin smiled over his shoulder. "We haven't seen you here at the castle in quite a while."

Before he could reply, his mother caught sight of him. Queen Kelby loved the water-filled castle and spent most of her time there. She looked much like Lorelei with an angelfish tail and bright blonde hair.

The Queen's beauty, however, was sophisticated and graceful. She wore an elaborate pearl and conch-shell crown and a wispy golden robe, the hem weighted down with rows of pearls. Long strands of graduated pearls encircled her neck.

Six well-dressed mermaids swam behind her, a constant presence for as long as he could remember. They all came from the noble families of the Southern Silver Isles and had been his mother's closest friends when she was a child. Each of them gave him a cool look and he suddenly wished he had remembered to wear a shirt.

"Dover? What a surprise." She gave him a small smile, but didn't rush to hug him. It had been three months since he last saw her.

Shauna would hug me and lecture me about visiting more, he thought. No. Shauna wouldn't have let three months pass.

"I've heard the mating call," he blurted out, then

flushed and covered his mouth. He hadn't meant to be so blunt.

Queen Kelby arched an eyebrow. "And?"

Dover gave her a confused look. "And I need to go find him."

His mother sighed. "Dover, royalty doesn't heed the mating call. Your marriage will be arranged by your father and Lord Eades." She paused. "Well, unless the call led you to someone in one of the noble families. Has it?"

Dover looked at the sandy floor, watching a hermit crab walk under his tail. "No."

"Then, there's no need to worry about the mating call." Queen Kelby nodded firmly. "You should, however, worry about your wardrobe. The necklace is nice, but you aren't even wearing your crown, Dover."

"Your Majesty," Ervin bowed deeply. "If I may, I'll escort the young prince to the treasury and fetch his crown. I do believe he left it there."

"Very well," Queen Kelby said, and nodded at them before swimming past with her constant escort.

Ervin waited until they had turned the corner before pulling Dover into a small niche. "You've heard the mating call? Where is it taking you?"

Dover smiled shakily. "Northwest. It doesn't matter, though. Right?"

"Wrong," Ervin said, voice hard. "The mating call is a sacred gift from our goddess. Not everyone hears it, and those that do, must honor the sea and follow the call."

Dover blinked. Ervin *never* spoke against the King and Queen. "What are you saying?"

Ervin looked sad for a moment. "It's not common knowledge, Your Highness, and I trust you will keep it to yourself, but your mother heard the mating call after she was engaged to your father. Her family insisted she ignore it, so she did. She has been a loyal wife to your father, but you know your parents, bluetail."

Dover swished his tail in agitation. His parents were hardly ever together in public and when they were, there were no displays of affection. "Does Father know?"

"Yes." Ervin sighed. "There is very little freedom in a position of power. Your father needed a queen, and your mother wanted the position."

Dover didn't have to ask why his father needed a queen. He needed as many children as possible to carry on their bloodline in case one or two were killed off. *Stupid fucking Sea Witch curse.*

"Would Father understand? If I went and told him?"

Ervin blew out a stream of bubbles. "No. Lord Eades is having too much fun searching for your future spouse."

Dover scowled. "Why does he focus on me?" Ten of his twelve siblings were unmarried, including the heir, his sister Talia.

Ervin's eyes grew cold. "I have my suspicions and fervently hope they aren't true." His expression softened. "Don't worry about that now. You need to find your mate. Your father's assistant told me the King expects you to move here by the end of the month, so that doesn't give you much time."

Dover bit his lip. "Shauna said she'd help me."

Ervin grinned. "Good. I won't ask any more questions. The less I know the better. Just make sure you are mated by the end of the month. A claimed mate is sacrosanct to all species, and Lord Eades will simply have to suck it up."

Dover smiled wide. "I, uh, have to go."

Ervin chuckled. "Let's get your crown first. I told your mother we would."

They swam to the treasury entrance, shifting as they left the water. A guard handed Dover a sarong and he knotted it at his waist.

Ervin waited for him patiently. All the servants wore plain black sarongs whether they wore their tail or their legs. Searching for clothes took time that they simply didn't have.

They walked into the huge vaulted room and Dover sighed happily. "So many shinies."

A deep chuckle drew his attention to the back. His brother Kai stood with Talia next to the display of crowns. "It's nice to see you, little brother."

Talia smiled nervously. "Are you moving in already? I was sure you would treasure the month Father gave you."

"No," Dover shook his head hard. "I just have to get my crown."

Talia tried to hide her grin. "You, Kai, and Kit are the only princes I know that hate wearing crowns. I still remember getting my first one." Her red hair was as bright as Kit's, and her crown of chocolate pearls and tulip shells was only a little smaller than Queen Kelby's.

Kai plucked a slender band of white seashells and polished white coral. "Here it is."

"Thanks." Dover put it on his head and grunted, hating the weight. "What are you two doing here?"

Talia scowled. "The Coalswells are being obnoxious. We're picking out some trinket to send their king."

"Why are they upset this time?" Dover had only met a few of the merfolk from the Northern Silver Isles. Their capital was Coalswell Tides and rumor said it was a dark and nasty place.

"Father is attempting to arrange a peace treaty with them," Kai said, shaking his head. "It seems pointless since King Nerio is as stubborn as Father, and I hear his son isn't much better."

"To seal the treaty, the Coalswells are insisting on a marriage between their prince and one of Father's children," Talia said.

"Why would Father not agree with that?" Dover scratched his head under his crown. He really hoped he didn't lose it again. It was always embarrassing when someone found it and brought it to Ervin.

"The Coalswells insist that Prince Tack gets to choose his prince or princess." Kai patted Talia on the back. "He'll choose Talia, then suddenly the Silver Isles are united under his rule."

Dover made a face. "Why his rule? Talia could take over everything."

His eldest sister grinned. "Hell yeah, I could."

Kai laughed. "Father doesn't want to take the chance."

"Politics." Dover groaned. "I don't want to leave my creek and waterfall."

Talia snorted. "There are times I wish I could go live with you."

Dover laughed. "You're always welcome." His laughter died suddenly. "Well, at least for another month."

Kai winced and picked up a delicate gold lariat necklace with a large heart-cut emerald pendant. He handed it to Talia. "This will work."

Talia gave him one more smile, then left. He could picture her summoning her red and white striped lionfish tail and swimming straight to the throne room. Their father usually met with the Coalswells there.

Dover squeaked when Kai pulled him into a hug. His eldest brother wasn't exactly the touchy-feely type. "I'm sorry Lord Eades has targeted you, little brother. Talia and I are trying to talk Father out of this whole mess."

"Thanks." Dover awkwardly patted Kai's back.

Kai stepped back. "Come on. I'll swim you home."

Dover looked behind him and Ervin smiled at him and nodded. "I'll see you soon, Prince Dover."

Dover was happy that Kai wanted to swim with him, but he kind of wished he wasn't there, so Dover could get a hug from Ervin.

Kai and he left the treasury, but they stopped for a few minutes for Kai to talk to the guards. Dover's brother would most likely be Talia's general once she became Queen of the Southern Silver Isles. He was a fierce warrior and utterly loyal to his family.

Eventually they reached the waterline and summoned their tails. Kai's tiger-shark tail had dark-brown stripes that matched his hair and eyes. A strip of rubbery tiger-shark skin ran down the middle of his back to meet the top of his tail.

Kai could swim much faster than Dover but kept it slow as they left the castle and swam toward the mouth of the Isles River. This route had more traffic, but at least he didn't have to go back to the royal beach.

"I notice you haven't been to the council meetings in months." Kai swam with a predatory grace that Dover tried to emulate.

"There's no reason for me to go." Dover hated those meetings. Lord Eades led them and the head of each of the noble families attended. The point of the meetings was to advise King Ren on policy revision, or as it really was, they advised the King to *not* revise any policies.

"Father has been listening to Lord Eades' advice lately, so Talia and I are trying to be more vocal," Kai said. "We want everyone in the kingdom to have a voice. That means you too."

Dover reached out and tugged his brother's dorsal fin. "No one hears my voice, Kai. There's no point in even trying."

Eventually the brackish water turned to fresh water. A sleek shape swam toward them, and a few seconds later Chubber plastered his chubby brown body to Dover's back.

Kai smiled, eyes soft. "I thought your otter stayed in your pond."

"It's not a pond," Dover said, scowling. "It's a creek and waterfall."

"Sorry." Kai didn't look very sorry.

"Chubber usually goes where I go. He's my companion." Something shiny caught his eye and Dover slowed and swam toward the bottom of the riverbed. "Oh, that pebble is so pretty."

The small rock was smooth and a very light blue. Dover picked it up and admired it for a moment. It would look perfect with his collection. But… he turned to find Kai watching him fondly and held the pebble out. "Here. This is for you."

Kai looked surprised. "Oh. Thanks, Dover."

"It may not be a fancy gem, but it's just as pretty as one."

"It's beautiful," Kai agreed, nodding, and Dover thought Kai might be telling the truth.

"What else is happening at court?" Dover asked, as they started swimming again.

His creek was one of many that connected the Isles River to one of the large lakes that were scattered around the inland of the main island. They would swim together until they reached Dover's waterfall. Then Dover would have to take the stairs that lined the cliff to get home since Kai didn't like it when he jumped off the top of the waterfall.

"The pearl farms are doing well," Kai said. "Lord Eades keeps pushing Father to expand the farms closer to the Deep."

Dover shuddered. "That's not a good idea."

Kai's face grew hard. "No, it's not. One curse from the Sea Witch six generations ago is still haunting our kingdom. The Deep should be avoided. Fortunately, Father is standing firm on that."

The Deep was a large and very deep trench that separated the Northern and Southern Silver Isles. The merfolk that inhabited the Deep were tentacle tailed and very elusive. Dover had always wondered how they lived down in their trench, but he was neither curious nor stupid enough to go ask.

"Tourism is up in Latch Bay too," Kai continued. "Father still won't let it expand to the rest of the islands, but at least he's letting humans into Latch Bay now. The nobles don't want the rest of the world to think Father is speciesist."

"I don't understand why he hates humans so much." Dover wrinkled his nose, then spotted Romeu swimming beneath him. "Crocodile shifters are so much worse."

The huge scaly saltwater crocodile beneath him whacked him with his tail and he giggled.

Kai glared at the shifter and drew his blade. "How dare you touch a prince."

Dover groaned and pushed his brother. "Romeu is my friend, Kai. We were just playing."

Romeu dipped his head, then swam quickly in the opposite direction.

Kai flushed. "I'm sorry, Dover. Will you offer him my apologies?"

"Sure. He likes to come sulk in my creek when his

wife kicks him out of the house so she can bake in peace. He says chocolate chips are like an aphrodisiac to him."

Kai laughed. "You make the most interesting friends."

∼

THE NEXT MORNING, Dover ran around the house, shoving his favorite shinies into a waterproof knapsack.

"Don't forget to pack clothes, bluetail," Shauna said, as she diced up papaya. "We have one hour before the ship leaves."

"I can't believe you talked someone into sneaking one of King Ren's sons off the isles." Nami carefully helped Chubber pack his own little bag full of pebbles.

"The ship's captain is a friend." Shauna blushed lightly.

Nami and Dover exchanged looks. "Shauna? How good of a friend is this ship's captain?"

"That's absolutely none of your business, now is it?"

"No, ma'am," he mumbled.

Shauna laughed. "Good boy. Now, George will get you to the United States. He's heading to South Carolina and will guide you wherever the call takes you after he's checked in with his niece."

"You have money, right? What about your passport?" Nami strapped Chubber's bag around the otter. "Oh, yeah. I meant to ask. Why is Chubber wearing your crown around his waist?"

Dover shrugged. "It got stuck. I don't think I have a passport or any cash."

Shauna shook her head. "Check the bookshelf in your bedroom, bluetail. That's where all your important papers are. Nami, help me get Dover's crown off Chubber."

They barely made it to the Latch Bay docks in time to catch the ship. Dover pulled his hat down to hide his face, then shoved Chubber back down into his shirt.

"I don't know why I can't go with him," Nami said, close to tears. "Mom, he's never been off the isles. Are you sure we can trust this man?"

Dover narrowed his eyes. "You haven't been off the isles either."

Shauna patted each of them on the shoulder. "It will be alright, Nami. You need to stay here and help cover for Dover, and I would trust George with my life. Do you really think I'd send our bluetail out into the world alone?"

Nami sighed. "No. I just don't want to say goodbye." She hugged Dover. "I'm going to miss you while you're gone."

Dover's eyes watered and he struggled not to cry. Nami and he had been best friends since they were babies.

An older beaver shifter approached and Dover let go of Nami. Shauna hugged him next and handed him a small cooler. "I packed your favorites in there. Eat it quick and don't hesitate to ask George for help if you need it. He truly is a good man."

"I'll keep an eye on your boy, Shauna." George

nodded to him and grinned. "Do you know anything about ships, kid?"

Dover blinked. "Uh, they float?"

George laughed. "This will be fun. Come on aboard, sailor."

CHAPTER 4

a week after the party, Ben finally had a couple of days off. Hurricane season usually slowed the tourists down a bit and the restaurant staff could finally take a deep breath and relax.

"Otis, you want to go fishing?"

Ben's dog tilted his head and grinned. "Woof."

"Let's go. Maybe we can catch something tasty for dinner." Ben gathered up his fishing gear and packed some water and snacks for the two of them. The marina was about a mile away and Ben stored his small fishing boat there.

Ben and Otis took their time walking down the private beach. As they passed Hester's house, Ben saw the witch napping on her back deck. Her familiar, Nettle, lounged on the railing. The cat watched him with wise eyes that sent a shiver down his back.

Nettle waited until they were in front of the house, then gave a god-awful screech.

Hester startled at the loud noise, waking up and looking around.

"Meow."

"Fuck, I almost missed him. Thanks, Nettle." Hester hopped out of her deck chair and waved her arms. "Ben, Otis needs to stay with me today."

Ben frowned. He had been promising Otis a fishing day for two weeks now. "Why?"

Hester gave him a stern look and settled her hands on her hips. "Because I said so. Otis, come here, boy."

Otis looked at him and Ben reluctantly nodded. He knew Hester had to have a good reason. The curly haired dog ran to Hester, then woofed softly at Nettle.

"Do I need to stay home?" Ben didn't much want to fish without Otis. He'd call Eloise, but her uncle had docked in Port Charleston yesterday and was driving down today for a visit.

"No," Hester hesitated for a moment. "No. You go on. We can't change things too much, now can we?"

Ben gave her a dry look. "Am I supposed to answer that?"

Hester chuckled. "Go have fun, Benny. I'll take care of Otis."

Ben finished the walk to the marina alone. He waved at a few familiar faces along the way, but kept to himself like usual.

His boat was small, just about twenty-five feet long, but he never went too far offshore in it. After uncovering the boat and refueling, He headed away from the marina and smiled, enjoying the salty air and the bright sunlight. He had really needed this.

He liked the simple repetition of his job, but he didn't like the lack of windows back in the dish room. He wished he could work outdoors, but there weren't a lot of jobs around town.

Gotta work to pay the bills, he thought with a shrug.

About ten miles away from shore, he baited some lines and tossed them into the water, before slowly steering the boat south. This was one of his favorite ways to fish offshore.

A few hours later, Ben had caught a twenty-pound Mahi Mahi and three average-sized mackerel. He looked up at the sky. He was enjoying the peace and quiet, but clouds were gathering for what looked like a late afternoon storm and he didn't want to be there when it arrived. He stored the fish in a cooler in the small engine cubby and started home.

He was five miles from the marina when the storm hit. One moment the sea was rocky, but manageable, and the next moment a massive wave crashed over his ship. He kept his footing and pushed forward, trying to keep the boat steady.

The second wave brought something with it, likely a bottle or some other debris. All Ben remembered was the pain as something struck his head. Then he was in the water, sinking beneath the waves as the salt stung his eyes and his vision dimmed.

Before he lost consciousness, Ben saw him – a blue-tailed angel.

THE STATIC-FILLED VOICE on the radio woke Ben. "You'll be fine, kid. The storm's dying down, and we have your coordinates. I have my niece's fishing boat. I'm coming to get you."

"He's bleeding all over the place, George." The voice sounded close to tears. "I just found him."

"See what you can do to stop the bleeding. We'll be there soon."

Ben moved his head and pain shot through him. "Fuck."

A young man moved into his eyesight. The slender, well-muscled stranger was completely naked with smooth, sun-kissed skin and dark blue hair. His eyes were full of tears and Ben reached out, not liking the idea of the man crying.

"You're going to be alright. George said so and he knows everything about everything." The young man knelt beside him. "The storm's over and your catch is still here. All the stuff on the deck went over though."

Ben moaned when the man lifted his head and put a life jacket under it. "Where did you come from?" He remembered a blue and silver tail whipping through the churning water.

The man blinked. "Uh, I fell... No, I jumped from a plane and landed during the storm. Then I saw you fall off your boat. Shew, I'm happy you were here or I'd just be floating around."

Ben tried not to laugh, knowing it would make his head feel worse. The merman was a horrible liar. "I didn't think any merfolk lived around here."

The man swallowed. "I wouldn't know about that.

I'm human. See my human legs?" He stretched out one of his bare legs and wiggled his toes, but Ben's eyes were drawn to the semi-hard dick between the man's legs.

"Why are you naked if you're human?"

The stranger whined and Ben felt guilty for pushing the merman to reveal something he obviously didn't want to. "My clothes were heavy when I landed, so I took them off."

Ben gave him a half-smile. "Okay. My name is Ben."

The man practically glowed with happiness and mouthed *Ben* silently.

"What's your name?"

"Oh, yeah. I'm Dover." He looked around the tiny cabin. "I like your boat, or is it called a ship? George got mad when I called his ship a boat, but I don't know why."

Ben smiled softly. "It's a boat."

Dover lifted the lid on the cooler under the small bench and gave a little wiggle. "I like Mahi Mahi. I'll grill it for you when we get home. It's really good with this pineapple sauce I make. You'll love it. Oh, where do you live? Is there water nearby? Do you like otters? Chubber will be upset if you don't."

"Chubber?" Ben's eyes were stuck on Dover's plump ass cheeks.

Dover looked over his shoulder and grinned. "He's my friend."

Ben flushed and raised his eyes to Dover's face. "He likes otters?"

"Chubber *is* an otter."

Ben's eyes felt heavy, but he did his best to follow the conversation. "He's a shifter?"

"Nope. Just the best otter in all the world. He doesn't like saltwater or he'd have been here too." Dover stood up and looked out the window, bouncing on his toes. "I see George! At least, I think that's George. *The Wet Beaver* is written on the side of the boat, and George is a beaver, so it must be him. Wait. *The Wet Beaver?*"

"Eloise," Ben managed to say before his eyes closed again.

WHEN HE WOKE AGAIN, he was in a hospital room. Dover stood next to the window with an older man Ben didn't recognize. Unfortunately someone had found some clothes for the merman.

"Isn't he the most handsome man you've ever seen, George?" Dover wiggled in place. "His eyes are like my favorite coffee. I really like coffee, George."

The man chuckled. "I'm aware, kid."

Dover pressed his hands to his cheeks and pushed them up. "His cheekbones are so sharp, and he's brown all over. I checked."

"Dover! Is that why he was naked when we got there?"

Dover gave George a stubborn look. "I had to make sure he didn't have any other injuries."

"For the love of birch trees, son, you act like you've never seen a man before."

Dover rolled his eyes and Ben struggled not to laugh. "Men are just men. Ben is perfection. Did you *see* his shoulders?"

Movement to his left made him turn his head and he winced at the pain it caused. Eloise sat in a chair beside him, her round chin propped on her fist.

"Uncle George won't tell me who the rando is or where he came from," Eloise whispered. "He's obsessed with you."

"He's not a rando. He's Dover."

"Dover, huh?" Eloise smirked. "I take it this is going to be a mutual obsession?"

Ben thought of blue tails and dark eyes. "Yeah. Definitely mutual."

"Ben? Are you awake?" Dover ran to his side and took his hand. "The doctor said you were okay, but you have a concussion. You get to go home tomorrow, and I'm going to watch over you to make sure you're really okay."

Ben thought maybe he should have minded a stranger inviting himself over, but it was Dover. He was *supposed* to go home with Ben. That's just how it was.

"You want to sit up?" Eloise asked.

"Yeah."

Dover and Eloise helped him sit up and his stomach started churning. Dover grabbed a wastebasket just in time to hold it as Ben puked. *Nice impression I'm making here.*

Eloise took George back to her house and promised to check on Otis, but Dover never left Ben's side. The young man sat by his bedside, looking decidedly grumpy. "Who's this Otis everyone keeps talking about?"

Ben hid a smile. "He's my dog."

Dover's eyes widened and he smiled excitedly. "A dog? I've never played with a dog before. Does he like water? Do you think he'll hurt Chubber?"

"Chubber?"

"Remember," Dover said, biting his lip. "I told you. Chubber's my friend. He's a river otter."

A sleek furry brown face peeked over the top of Dover's loose, buttoned-up jacket. The otter chirped quietly and watched Ben.

Ben blinked. "Uh, you brought him into the hospital."

Dover frowned, eyes sad. "I couldn't leave him outside by himself."

Ben didn't like the vulnerability on Dover's face. "Hi, Chubber."

The little otter chirped again and wiggled under Dover's shirt. "Be still, Chubber," Dover whispered, then gave Ben a concerned look. "He's just a baby so he doesn't listen too well."

Ben's eyes were getting heavy again. "Why isn't he with his mom?"

Dover blushed. "His mom is a friend of mine. I met him right after he was born and he decided he was mine. Shell doesn't mind too much. She has plenty of pups."

"What about your family?" Ben asked, even as his eyes closed.

"You should get some sleep," he heard Dover say.

~

THE NEXT MORNING Ben sat in the passenger side of Eloise's car, trying not to laugh as his best friend and Dover fought over who would help him from the car.

Dover shoved Eloise to the side. "I'll help him."

Eloise glared and hip bumped Dover away from the door. "He's *my* best friend. I'll help him."

Dover gasped. "Your big butt won't stop me. Move over."

"My butt is *not* big you blue-haired fish face." Eloise shoved Dover, then screeched when Chubber popped out of the man's jacket to hiss at her.

George sighed. "Come on, Ben. I'll help you to the house."

Ben grinned. "I'm really okay. I just like watching those two fight."

Dover and Eloise glared at one another, not even noticing when Ben got out of the car. They started circling one another.

George chuckled. "Eloise is a suspicious one, that's for sure. She'll settle down once she gets to know Dover. He's a sweet young man." He steadied Ben as they walked toward the house.

"You pulled my hair," Eloise yelled. "The son of a bitch actually pulled my hair!"

Hester met them at Ben's door, Otis at her side. Ben's dog barked and started running around Ben and George.

45

"Otis is happy to see you." Hester gave him a sad look. "He wouldn't have made it, you know. If he had gone with you yesterday."

Ben slowly knelt down and hugged the golden doodle. "Thank you, Hester. I don't know what I'd do without him." He looked up. "Why didn't you tell me not to go?"

The witch shrugged and nodded toward where Dover still squabbled with Eloise. Chubber now perched on her head, tugging her hair in his little paws, while Dover tried to dodge Eloise's slaps.

Hester chuckled. "Some things need to happen. You'll thank me later."

Dover froze in the middle of pinching Eloise's side. "Is that Otis? Oh, he's so cute. Chubber, isn't he cute?"

Chubber paused and looked at the dog. He tilted his head and chirped curiously.

Otis watched the small otter carefully. "Woof."

Chubber immediately let go of Eloise's hair and jumped from her head, scurrying over to Otis. He stood on his back legs and patted Otis' face. Ben thought he must like what he saw. The otter gurgled, then climbed on top of Otis' back. He lay flat, then started to purr.

Dover clapped, then hugged Eloise, surprising the woman. "Look! They like each other."

Eloise wrinkled her nose, but let Dover hug her. Her eyes met Ben's over the merman's head. "Your man is weird."

CHAPTER 5

*D*over pushed Eloise away and hurried to Ben's side, maneuvering under his arm and against his side. "I have you, Ben. Let's get you inside so you can relax."

An older woman with long grey and brown hair watched him, eyes shining with happiness. "I'm glad you finally made it here, bluetail."

Dover yipped, eyes wide. *How does she know my nickname?*

"I'm Hester," she said. "Don't you go worrying about me saying something, kid. I know when to keep my mouth shut, and George here is a good friend."

Ben blinked sleepily. "What are you talking about?"

"Nothing," Dover said quickly, and helped his mate through the doorway. He leaned up and sniffed Ben as they walked. *Smells so good!*

"Bluetail, huh? It fits. Why are you sniffing Ben?" Eloise asked.

Dover stuck his tongue out at her. The beaver

shifter reminded him of Nami. He missed his best friend so much and it had only been a week.

Eloise laughed and pushed past them. "Stewart and Ryan checked over your boat, Ben, and brought your catch home. They cleaned it and put it in the freezer."

"Thanks," Ben said, and Dover shivered. His mate's voice was deep and husky.

So delicious, he thought, then gasped, distracted by all the wonderful shinies around the room.

Ben's beach cottage was simple and cozy, but that wasn't what caught Dover's eyes. All around the room were pieces of the most exquisite glass art. There were vines made of tiny bits of green glass hanging from the ceiling in front of the windows. Hidden within them were small, colorful glass flowers. There were pretty vases made of broken pieces of glass and metal, and small blown glass figurines sitting on tables and bookshelves.

The most beautiful piece of all hung above the couch. The ocean with a large wave curling at the top was framed in driftwood and made of hundreds of shards of glass in various blues. Brown and white bits formed the shapes of starfish at the bottom of the picture and a pretty blue shell sat nestled among green strands of kelp.

Dover felt the sting of homesickness, but pushed it away as he helped Ben sit on the comfy-looking couch. Otis, with Chubber on his back, hopped up on the couch beside Ben and settled his head on the human's knee.

Ben stroked the dog's silky ears. "Sorry for the scare, buddy."

Dover plastered himself to Ben's other side and pet Otis too. "Hi, Otis. I'm Dover and this is Chubber. It's nice to meet you."

Otis gave him a doggy smile, then closed his eyes.

"Smart doggy," Dover said. "You should rest a bit while I unpack."

Ben leaned his head against the back of the couch and closed his eyes, a smile stretched across his face. "Yes, sir."

Eloise narrowed her eyes. "Why are you unpacking?"

Dover slowly slid out of his seat, careful not to disturb Ben and Otis. He pulled Eloise into the kitchen, hoping Ben would sleep. "I have to take care of Ben," he whispered to Eloise. "Duh."

"The doctor said he would be fine with a little rest," Eloise said, hands on her hips. "There's no reason for you to stay. You're just some stranger."

Dover's lip trembled. He *was* just some stranger. A stranger that was a long way from everything familiar.

"Fuck," Eloise said, groaning. "Don't look like that. I'm sorry, alright? Damn it, you act like you two are mates... *Oh.*"

Dover gave her a panicked look. "You can't say anything, okay? I don't want him to run screaming and George said humans are kinda odd about mates."

Eloise rubbed her hands over her face. "They normally are. They don't mingle well with other species. Hell, other species don't mingle well either. My

49

little brother married an omega vampire and I thought Mom was going to murder him."

Dover's lip trembled again. "His family won't like me?"

Eloise patted his shoulder. "They don't like Ben, so I wouldn't worry about it. Hester and I are Ben's family. He has a few friends in the area, but they'll like you too."

Dover snarled. "What's wrong with his family? Why don't they like him? He's perfection and all things beautiful."

Eloise snorted. "Holy oak trees, you're just sad."

"Eloise," Dover said sternly, glaring at the woman.

"Okay, so his parents don't like that he's gay, because they're Beta Fundamentalists. They're all *man goes with woman* and that's it. They obviously hate alpha women and omega men too, so I wouldn't even try with them." Eloise shrugged. "He hasn't talked to them in years."

Dover knew some people were resentful of alpha women for being able to impregnate others and omega men for being able to get pregnant. Hell, Lord Eades hadn't made his own disgust with them a secret.

If the Beta Fundamentalist Church had a branch in the Silver Isles, Lord Eades would be a member of it. Dover kinda looked forward to seeing Eades' face when Talia inherited the throne.

Dover hopped up to sit on the kitchen counter. "Family can be complicated."

"Tell me about it." Eloise snorted. "My parents don't like Uncle George because he decided to captain a ship instead of going into construction like the rest of us. They think all beavers should stick to building."

"George is a really good captain," Dover said. "He brings people all over the world and has lots of shiny things in his cabin."

Eloise arched a brow. "Where did he find you?"

Dover gave her a blank look. "Uh, South America?"

"Hey, kid," George said, grabbing Eloise's attention. "I put your bags in the hallway."

Dover jumped off the counter and bounced over to the man to hug him. "Thank you, George. Did you get Chubber's bag too?"

"I did. Don't want the little guy to be without his stash. I'm gonna pretend that I don't know he stole my watch." George chuckled. "It's an old one anyway. Got it in Cairo twenty years ago."

Dover winced. "Sorry about that. I'll pay you for it."

George hugged him back. "Don't worry about it. I'll take Eloise and we'll get out of your way."

"I still have questions," Eloise said grumpily.

"I know it's a hard thing to do, but mind your own business," George said, shaking his head. "Hester told me something interesting about you."

Eloise looked startled. "What?"

George started toward the front door. "You'll have to come with me to find out."

Eloise groaned, but followed her uncle outside.

Dover smiled. He really loved George.

He peeked into the living room and saw that Ben was stretched out on the couch sleeping. Otis slept on top of Ben's stomach and legs, and Chubber curled up on his chest.

"Time to snoop," he whispered and grabbed his bag.

Dover walked through Ben's home, admiring all the glass art. The small house had two bedrooms. He walked into Ben's bedroom and sighed happily. Everything smelled like his human. He set his bag down and jumped on the large bed, giggling as he bounced. He buried his face in Ben's pillow and sniffed deeply.

I'm sleeping right here tonight, he thought. Dover knew he should try to take things slowly so his mate could get to know him, but he didn't want to. All he wanted was to be near Ben. His mate was so handsome with his dark skin and bouncy curls, and his smile turned Dover's heart to mush.

It had frightened him to see Ben fall into the sea during the storm, and he had never been so happy to be an impulsive stalker. When George and he had arrived at Eloise's house, the mating call had pulled Dover straight to the ocean. He had seen his human fall in and immediately dragged him back to the storm-tossed boat.

"Never again," Dover whispered against the pillow. "I'll protect my Ben forever."

He reluctantly climbed out of bed and took a few minutes to unpack his bag. He probably should have packed more clothes, but he had wanted to bring his favorite shinies with him.

He hung a few around the room and spread his jewels across the top of the old, chipped dresser before going to explore the rest of the small beach house. The other bedroom looked like a workshop. There was a wooden desk covered with notebooks, pencils, compasses, and a laptop.

Over by the window was a large metal table with all types of tools on it that Dover didn't recognize. There were also markers and little bottles that looked like paint.

Besides that, the room was full of boxes and shelves that were covered with bits of glass and driftwood.

"My mate's an artist," he said quietly, feeling overwhelmed knowing that Ben was responsible for the beautiful glass art pieces that decorated the house. "I'm so lucky."

He reached into his pocket and pulled out his favorite pearl. It was a perfectly round, greyish-blue freshwater pearl. As a prince, he had full access to the royal treasury and his mother often pressured him to take and wear some of the beautiful, but elaborate, sets of jewelry.

He had never found any of his shinies in the royal treasury.

Ben's voice came from behind him. "Hey, Dover. Are you okay? I'm sorry the place is so messy. I wasn't expecting company."

Dover spun around. "You're supposed to be sleeping."

Ben grinned, looking exhausted. "Had to take a piss. What's that?"

Dover tugged the big alpha into the room and pushed him into the well-cushioned chair next to the window. Ben leaned back and gave him a curious look.

Dover held out his favorite pearl. "This is my favorite treasure."

Ben took it and held it up to the light. "It's beautiful, Dover. I don't know a lot about pearls. What kind is this?"

"It's a Southern Silver Isles freshwater pearl. It's small and one of the most inexpensive varieties," Dover said, and scooted into Ben's lap. "When I was really little, three of my sisters were making fun of me. They called me mean names and pulled my tai... toe. They pulled my toe. Anyway, I ran away and holed up in a storage room to cry."

Ben cupped his face, and Dover leaned into his hand. "Your sisters sound like assholes."

"Some are mean, some just don't care." Dover shifted closer, enjoying the feel of Ben's hard thighs beneath him. "Anyway, one of the, uh, one of my father's employees found me. Ervin picked me up and hugged me until I stopped crying. When I told him what they said, he kissed my head and told me that being beautiful wasn't about how I looked. He said the rarest pearl in the Silver Isles would only bring joy to a person that truly treasured it. He told me my sisters didn't know how to treasure anything."

"Or anyone," Ben whispered, nuzzling Dover's ear.

"Ervin had a string of pearls that his mate gave him on their wedding day." Dover sniffled. "He told me that those pearls didn't cost a lot of money, but he treasured them more than pure gold. His mate had collected each one himself, then strung them together."

"It was a gift of love," Ben said.

Dover nodded, pleased that Ben understood. "Ervin treasured them because he knew they symbolized his mate's love. He pulled one off the strand and gave it to me and said that he knew how to properly treasure people and he would teach me too."

Ben's voice was starting to sound sleepy again. "He sounds like a smart man."

"He's the best ever. He introduced me to Shauna and Nami and I love them more than anything," Dover said, leaning his head against Ben's shoulder. "I miss them, but one day you'll get to meet them. Shauna will really like you."

Ben gave him a solemn look. "Are you sure? I'm not much, Dover."

Dover blinked several times, confused. "Ben, look around you. Look at all the pretty broken pieces you've collected. You know how to treasure. Even if I didn't already know you were perfect, this room and your art would tell me everything I needed to know."

Ben's dark eyes started to drift shut. "Who are you, Dover?"

"I'll tell you later, okay?" Dover slipped his pearl into the small pocket on the front of Ben's button-up shirt while the alpha's eyes were closed.

Ben ran a hand over Dover's back. "Whatever you need, bluetail."

CHAPTER 6

*T*he next day, Ben hummed as he smoothed the edges of the shard of glass in front of him. This part of his work was a bit tedious, and it took patience to refurbish the broken pieces of glass he found on the beach, or picked up at the local dump. The end product made it worth the work.

Dover sat sideways in the chair nearby, legs hanging over one side as he read one of Ben's books. The merman wore a bright blue sarong and nothing else. Ben had noticed Dover didn't care much for clothes. Ben was okay with that.

Ben patted his shirt pocket, smiling when he felt Dover's pearl. The merman was something special. He had told him about his friends Shauna and Nami, and it broke Ben's heart to hear the sadness in his voice. The merman missed them and Ben didn't know what to do about it.

A squeak caught his attention and he looked down.

Chubber stood on his back legs and patted Ben's leg. "What do you have there, Chubber?"

The otter chirped and handed him a shiny green pebble.

"Chubber," Dover said, surprise filling his voice. "That's your favorite pebble."

Ben took the pebble and considered it. "I could use this in my next project. Are you sure you want to give it up?"

The otter chirped again and scrambled up his leg and stretched onto his shoulders before settling down with a purr.

"I didn't know otters purred," Ben said, turning to Dover.

Dover looked thoughtful. "Chubber really likes you."

Ben nodded to where Otis lay beside Dover's chair. "It's only fair. Otis likes you."

Dover laughed and leaned down to pet Otis' head. "I've never had a dog before. He's fun to play with and he's a good cuddler. He'd like my cottage."

Ben tilted his head. This wasn't the first time Dover had mentioned his cottage. Dover seemed to miss it as much as Shauna and Nami.

Ben considered the pieces lying in front of him. "Tell me about your waterfall, bluetail."

Dover leaned back, staring at the ceiling with a smile. "The crest width is about twenty feet and it falls about fifty feet into my creek. The water's so clean and cool. Chubber and I keep most of our shinies in the plunge pool, and there's plenty of room to swim and play. Chubber's mom comes and visits all the time. She lives in the beaver dam at the end of my creek."

Ben started visualizing what he wanted to create and grabbed his drawing pad. "How big is the creek?"

"Around the waterfall, it's probably about seventy feet," Dover said, frowning in thought. "It's stays nice and wide until it gets to Shell's dam. Then it narrows a bit until it meets the lake. Shauna and Nami live on the lake."

"Who is Shell?"

Dover grinned. "That's Chubber's mom. Now, the best thing about my creek is the fish. There are bluegill, bass, and catfish. There are also frogs and snails, but I don't eat them."

Ben grinned. Dover loved fish. He had grilled the Mahi Mahi and made some kind of tasty sauce to go with it. It had been damn good. "What about around the creek?"

Ben sketched as Dover spoke. He was almost certain Dover was from the Southern Silver Isles. He didn't understand why Dover thought he needed to hide it, but maybe it was because Ben was human.

According to the news, King Ren didn't care much for humans. That probably had to do with the Poaching Wars. It had been ten years since they had ended, but there had been a lot of damage to the reefs around the Silver Isles.

"Then you just follow the path and there's my cottage," Dover said, sighing.

Ben looked up from his sketchpad, a sudden lump in his throat. "How long until you go back?"

Dover blinked, looking confused. "Uh, I don't know. I like your home."

Ben snorted. "I noticed several new rocks, shells, and pearls around the house."

Dover yawned. "My shinies need space to breathe."

Ben had also noticed several pieces of jewelry laid out on his dresser. One particular piece was a five strand natural pearl necklace that had to be worth more than Ben's house.

"So, I was in the U.S. Marine Corps." Ben squinted and kept his eyes on his sketchpad.

"Really?" Dover moved from his chair to sit on the end of Ben's worktable. "You're a protector. I can see you as a marine."

Ben turned his sketchpad so Dover couldn't see it. He wanted this to be a surprise. "I knew a guy named Jay. He's a merman from Haverdell."

"Haverdell? There are merfolk there?" Dover sounded surprised.

"Jay said most mers live in the Silver Isles, but Haverdell is the most diverse place I've ever been. I've never seen so many species in one place before."

"I bet that's fun," Dover said, with a smile.

"I spent the holidays with Jay and his mom a few years ago," Ben mused. "It was interesting to say the least. Anyway, Jay said merfolk are usually pretty elusive. Outside of the Silver Isles, there are only a few small colonies and they're kind of insular."

Dover bit his lip. "I heard that too."

"I have no problem with any species," Ben said bluntly. "I learned a long time ago that there are

.W. GRAY

shitheads all over the world and their species wasn't what made them that way."

Dover's eyes were so dark a blue they looked black. "That's true. Alright, let's say there was a merman that came from the Silver Isles. What if his family didn't like humans?"

Ben set his sketchpad down and cupped Dover's face, stroking a thumb over his cheek. "If that was the case, I would only care what the merman thought about humans."

Dover leaned into his touch. "What if this merman liked humans and wanted to stay with one of them, but his family wouldn't like it?"

Ben had to push back a growl. Fuck Dover's family. "I would tell the merman that he could stay with his human as long as he wanted."

Dover grinned, then leaned forward, pressing his mouth to Ben's.

Ben groaned and tilted Dover's head to the perfect angle to deepen the kiss. His merman tasted like heaven.

Dover leaned back. "I'm a merman from the Southern Silver Isles."

Ben grinned and pulled him in for another kiss. "I know."

Chubber nipped Ben's ear, startling him, and Dover laughed. "He says no kissing while he's on your shoulders."

Ben frowned, trying to think of a nice way to remove the damn otter.

Dover giggled, then hopped off the worktable.

"Come on, Otis. Let's go for a swim. I'll watch out for you and we can look for seashells."

Otis woofed and stood, wagging his tail.

Ben watched them leave. He wanted to go too, but the glass was calling him. "Well, Chubber, it looks like it's just you and me."

The otter started purring again and Ben turned back to his worktable. His sketch was of Dover's waterfall and creek. He had some glass pieces, a pretty pebble, and a cherished pearl to work with. He didn't like that his omega was homesick.

"My omega," he said aloud, trying the words out. "Chubber, I shouldn't like the sound of that so much. I just met him."

Chubber snuggled against his neck and chirped.

"You're right." Ben started coloring in his sketch. "Dover and you fit here with Otis and me."

LATER THAT NIGHT Ben rested with Otis and Chubber on the couch and watched Dover cook dinner in the kitchen. Otis was worn out from swimming with Dover all day, but the two had brought Ben a very pretty scallop shell and a greyish blue tulip shell. He had also brought back a sack of clams.

"Do you think we can get some groceries tomorrow?" Dover asked, looking up from the frying pan. He was making fresh fried clam strips. "I can make a yummy clam chowder from the leftover clam meat, but I need some things."

"Sure. I shouldn't be so tired." Ben was a little surprised he was as worn out as he was just from a little head bump. *So much for being a tough marine*, he thought.

"You're recovering," Dover said, and narrowed his eyes. "You *will* rest and recover."

Ben smiled. "Yes, sir."

Dover sniffed. "So, I know you're an artist, but Eloise said something about you working in a restaurant."

"Yeah. I'm a dishwasher in a restaurant in town." Ben snorted when Chubber started playing with Otis' ears. His dog just kept on sleeping.

"Do you like working there?"

Ben looked up. "It's a job. I like my co-workers, though. They're good people."

"They're your friends?"

"I guess." Ben shrugged. "They aren't as close as Eloise."

"And Hester," Dover added. "She's a witch. Doesn't that make you nervous?"

Ben chuckled. "She's the local hedge witch, not a fairy-tale crone tossing out curses."

Dover shivered and Ben narrowed his eyes. *Hmm, my omega is afraid of witches.*

"Otis likes her, so I'll try to trust you two," Dover said, taking a deep breath. "Eloise told me that you don't get along with your family."

Ben winced. "Can't we talk about common hobbies or something? Uh, I work on my projects and fish. What about you?"

Dover scooped the fried clam strips from the pan and set them onto a towel. "I swim, collect shinies, and avoid my family."

"Family," Ben said with a sigh. "My mom and dad are beta fundamentalists. They think betas are the most balanced and superior gender, so any non-betas should pretend they're betas – straight betas."

Dover wrinkled his nose. "There are a few like that on the Silver Isles. Bigotry isn't speciesist."

"I have a sister and a brother that are just like them," Ben said. "My sister is an alpha, but basically pretends she's a beta."

"That is one good thing about my family," Dover said. "My parents don't seem to care if we're omega, beta, or alpha."

"What do they care about?" Ben pulled Chubber away from Otis' ears and set the otter on his chest. He would have to think about getting the little guy a pool or something.

Dover was quiet a minute. "They care about appearances. We're supposed to always be on our best behavior and look perfect. Since I have a guppy tail, I'm supposed to be quiet and blend in with the background. Hell, I've lost count of the number of times Mother has shushed me in front of people. She's afraid I'll say something stupid and embarrass her."

Ben growled. "Fuck that! I love hearing what you think and your tail is beautiful. What's wrong with having a guppy tail?"

Ben thought back to everything he knew about merfolk. Jay and his family had guppy tails. Ryan had a mermaid friend overseas that had a koi tail, but Ben didn't understand what the problem was. The way Dover glowed from the inside out made it obvious he was treasure. Couldn't his mother see that?

"They're common," Dover said. "The merfolk in the Silver Isles treasure their ancestry and try to keep their lines as unique as possible. I'm the only one in my entire family's history to have a guppy tail."

"I like your tail," Ben said. "I like *you*. You're the shiniest shiny around here."

Dover smiled wide and ran around the counter to jump in Ben's lap, dislodging Chubber. He gave Ben a deep, wet kiss before pulling back to watch him. "I know treasure when I see it too, Ben."

CHAPTER 7

"*B*en," Ryan said, grinning. "Your omega is outside. He has something to show you."

Ben looked up from the rack of dishes he was unloading. "Why are you smiling like that?"

Ryan just laughed. "Have I told you how great it is that Eloise and Dover are friends now?"

"What did she do?" Ben groaned, and took off his apron.

He was happy that Eloise and Dover got along now, but Eloise was an expert at trouble and Dover was too gullible for Ben's peace of mind. That was how they'd ended up with a dick-shaped fountain on the back deck. Chubber loved the thing, and Dover was proud of himself for finding it on clearance, so Ben couldn't complain.

Stewart cleaned his plates and put them in the bin. "Aww, look at that frown. Ben is worried about his snookums."

"More like he's worried he'll end up with a vulva-shaped hot tub," Ryan said, laughing.

Ben ignored them and hurried toward the back door. The past two weeks had been wonderful. Dover had settled in and spent his days with Ben and his afternoons swimming and seashell collecting with Otis and Chubber.

Ben liked seeing Dover sleeping in his bed when he got home from work. He liked holding his omega close as he fell asleep, even with Dover's soft snores. Ben didn't even mind cleaning up all the sand Dover carried in with him from the beach. He especially liked Dover's kisses.

They were getting along just fine, then Eloise had to stick her stupid beaver nose into their business. When she wasn't dragging Dover into trouble, she was trying to find the merman a job.

First, she had decided that Dover would work for her construction company. It hadn't gone well and Ben might have yelled a little too loudly when he'd seen the blisters on Dover's hands from carrying lumber all day.

After that, Eloise had decided that Dover would work at the grocery store, but apparently otters were a health code violation. They were also attracted to red hair and Mrs. Douglas could yell even louder than Ben when an otter jumped on her head.

After pacifying the manager of the grocery store, Eloise had decided that Dover would work in the factory one town over. That might have worked, except Dover didn't know how to drive, so Ryan had tried to teach him, and now Ben's truck had a nice-sized dent in the back bumper.

Ben was a little worried about what they had been up to today. It was only four in the afternoon. Surely it couldn't be that bad.

Behind the restaurant, Dover and Eloise stood next to a powder-blue Vespa with a sidecar. Otis sat in the sidecar with Chubber, a long, dark-blue scarf around his neck and a pair of goggles covering his eyes.

Dover danced in place, dressed only in his sarong and flip flops. Ben worried what the merman would do when it got colder. Dover *really* didn't like clothes.

"Isn't it the most beautiful thing you've ever seen?"

Eloise smirked. "I told him he could have it once he gets his license."

Dover grabbed Ben's hand and pulled him to the Vespa. "Eloise showed me how to drive it and said I did well. Just think, I could go to the grocery store and the marina, or even just go on a ride with Otis and Chubber. We could *all* go on a ride. You could ride your motorcycle and I would have my Vespa."

Eloise cackled. "Won't that be so much fun, Ben?"

Dover's hopeful expression was Ben's downfall. "Sure will, bluetail. We'll figure out how to get your license in the morning, okay?"

Dover jumped and Ben caught him in his arms, squeezing him tight. "You're the best, Ben. I'll make your favorite omelet for breakfast."

"Come on," Eloise said, pulling Dover off of Ben. "Ben needs to get back to work. You and I are going to Hester's for dinner."

Dover made a face. "Don't let her turn me into a frog, alright? I like frogs and all, but I can't kiss Ben if I'm a frog."

Eloise rolled her eyes and got onto the Vespa. "You say that each time we go to her house. She said she had a present for you, remember? That doesn't sound bad."

Dover kissed Ben's cheek then jumped behind Eloise and pulled his helmet on. "She could just be waiting for me to lower my guard."

Eloise sped away and Ben shook his head. "A fucking Vespa."

Muffled laughter came from the door to the restaurant. When he opened it, Stewart and Ryan almost fell out.

"Come on, Ben," Ryan said. "Did you really have any street cred left to lose? You ride around with Hester all the time."

Ben winced. "Good point."

The rest of the night went by quickly. He rode home and parked his bike next to the stupid Vespa. He unlocked the door, then shut it quietly behind him.

Dover always left him a snack in the kitchen, so Ben tiptoed across the living room. He really needed to try to change his shift so he'd have more time with Dover in the evening.

Ben had just sat down at the table to eat the grilled clam toasts when he heard tiny paws running down the hall from the bedroom.

A floppy eared, brown puppy skidded to a halt at the table and stared at him. It looked like a Boykin Spaniel, but Ben wasn't sure.

"Uh, hi." The puppy gave a very tentative woof. "I guess you're Hester's present, huh?"

"Ben?" Dover rubbed his eyes as he stumbled into the room, completely naked. "Did you meet Jojo?"

Ben smiled and pulled Dover into his arms. "Jojo?"

"Hester said she was rejected by her witch because she wanted a fancier familiar."

Ben frowned and leaned down to pick up the puppy. "Poor little girl."

"I know, right? Hester said Jojo wasn't meant for you or me, but we need to keep her until she finds her forever person." Dover blinked sleepily. "We'll help her find her people."

Ben smiled. "You have a good heart, Dover."

His omega snorted. "I'm a selfish twat. At least that's what Nami would say."

"Why? You're the furthest thing from selfish."

Dover's expression grew serious. "I miss you when you're gone to work. I want you to quit work and stay with me all day."

Ben nuzzled his neck. "I miss you too. Gotta pay the bills, though."

"Eloise wants me to have a job, so I'll stay," Dover said. "She's worried I'll get bored."

Ben's heart sped up at the thought of Dover leaving. Not happening. "Bored? Are you bored with me?"

Dover rolled his eyes. "That's impossible. I won't get bored, Ben. Eloise just worries. It makes her feel better to solve a problem even though there isn't a problem here."

Ben breathed a sigh of relief. He didn't think Dover

would appreciate being chased around the world, but Ben would do it if he had to. He was far too attached to the merman.

"Hester told me something at dinner." Dover sounded so defeated. "She told me that I couldn't stay here forever."

"Hester doesn't know shit. You can stay with me as long as you want."

Dover's eyes narrowed. "As long as I want? Promise?"

Ben kissed his forehead even as his stomach clenched in nervousness. He didn't know what he'd do if Dover left. He loved him. He loved the merman. "I promise."

"This is why I'm a selfish twat," Dover said and buried his face against Ben's neck, practically purring. "I miss Shauna and Nami, but I belong with you. It won't be easy."

"Fuck easy," Ben said and set Jojo back on the floor so he could hug Dover close. It was too early in their relationship for love, but he felt what he felt. "I want you, Dover... any way I can have you."

He ran a hand through Dover's hair and tilted his face up for a kiss. Dover moaned and shifted so that he straddled Ben and their cocks pressed together.

Ben's hands slid down Dover's back and cupped the omega's firm, plump ass.

"Your kisses are better than papaya," Dover said, licking Ben's bottom lip. He rocked his hips against Ben's.

Ben slid a finger down the crease in Dover's ass and tapped his hole. "Dover, can I..."

"Yes, yes, yes, yes," Dover said, and kissed Ben again. "Now. Right here."

Ben laughed and stood, Dover's legs wrapped around his waist. "How about the bed?"

Dover bit his neck, hard. "Hurry."

Jojo woofed and followed them to the bedroom before leaving them to go lie down with Otis and Chubber in the large dog bed.

Ben fell back on the bed, taking Dover with him. Damn, he loved this man so much. How had it happened so quickly? He had gone his whole life without feeling this, then suddenly, there it was. Like it some kind of fated shit.

Dover kissed his way down Ben's chest, pausing to nibble on each nipple. Ben stroked his fingers through Dover's hair, enjoying the wet heat of his omega's mouth.

A few moments later, Ben groaned and arched his hips when Dover swallowed his cock. "Damn it, I won't last, Dover."

He pulled Dover up his body and kissed him again. "Need lube. Hold on."

Dover growled and reached into the drawer on the nightstand. "I want you in me, Ben."

Ben twisted and rolled Dover over, grabbing the lube. "Anything for you."

He took his time exploring Dover's lean and muscular body, then pushed a lubed finger into Dover's hole. The omega spread his legs wide and angled his hips up, body writhing on the bed when Ben added two more fingers.

"Ben," Dover said, hands pulling Ben's face to his. "I'm gonna bite you, okay?"

Ben moved his body and lined his dick up with Dover's hole. He was about to find heaven, so Dover could do whatever he wanted to him. "Sure."

Ben pushed inside Dover at the same moment that tiny sharp teeth bit into his neck. It should have hurt, but fuck, the pleasure was almost too much. Heat flowed from his neck to his dick and he couldn't stop himself from pounding into Dover's ass.

Dover's teeth stayed latched onto Ben's neck and the merman growled as he moved with Ben. Dover's fingers dug into his mate's back, but Ben didn't care. Ben had never felt anything like this.

Seconds later, Ben came, eyes rolling up as he filled Dover's ass. He panted for a moment, then moaned when his dick started hardening again. "What the hell?"

Dover growled again and his teeth sent shards of intense pleasure shooting through Ben. "Mine," he mumbled through his bite.

Ben started moving again, pushing in and pulling out of Dover's ass as fast as he could. He was desperate for his omega. Moments later, he felt Dover come, splattering his stomach, and found his own release.

It didn't last long, and Ben started moving again. "Dover."

Dover's mouth clamped down again on Ben's neck. "Mine, mine, mine."

Ben came three more times before Dover's teeth

released his neck. His body shook and he braced his head against Dover's shoulder. "Holy shit."

Dover's eyes were black and a dreamy smile covered his face as he stroked a hand down Ben's back. "My Ben. My mate. You're all mine."

Ben nuzzled Dover's neck, confused. He was so tired. It felt like he'd run a thousand marathons and he felt sleep overtaking him. *Mate?*

CHAPTER 8

*D*over sang along to the radio in the kitchen as he cooked Ben's omelet. His mate was still sleeping, and Dover wanted to bring him breakfast in bed. Otis and Chubber were on the porch playing in the fountain, and Jojo sat on a pillow next to the refrigerator and howled along to the song. Dover didn't understand how anyone could *not* like the adorable puppy.

He finishing cutting the avocado and set the slices next to the tomatoes on the plate. After moving the dishes around on the tray, Dover carried the tray back to the bedroom, bouncing as he walked.

Ben was still sleeping stretched out on his stomach. Dover's mating heat had pulled a lot out of Ben. Dover giggled at his mental pun and Ben opened his eyes.

"I brought you breakfast," Dover said, climbing onto the bed. "It's your favorite kind."

Ben sat up and rubbed his eyes. "Thanks, love."

They sat across from each other and started eating.

Dover shoveled his food into his mouth as fast as he could. He had never been so hungry.

Ben slid some of his omelet onto Dover's empty plate and cleared his throat. "So, last night."

Dover swallowed his bite. "Yeah?"

"That wasn't normal." Ben rubbed the side of his neck where Dover's bite still showed.

Dover smiled smugly. His bite would leave a mating scar and everyone would know Ben was his. "You said I could stay with you forever."

Ben smiled softly. "Yeah, but that doesn't explain how I got hard that many times in a row. Is it always like that with merfolk?"

Dover stabbed a tomato, feeling a surge of jealousy. "You're mine! No thinking about sex with other people."

Ben snorted. "Dover. Tell me what the hell is going on."

Dover grabbed the last piece of toast from Ben's plate. "You're my mate. All mine."

Ben's mouth dropped open. "Why the fuck didn't I think of that? It explains so much."

"Eloise says humans are dense about mating," Dover said, shrugging. "I just didn't want you to run." He leaned forward and kissed Ben. "Now you're stuck with me. Forever."

Ben started to speak, then shut his mouth and thought a moment. "That should scare me, but the thought of being without you is more frightening."

"It's how it should be," Dover said, nodding. He

75

hoped he looked like he knew what the hell he was talking about.

"So what do we do now?" Ben asked. "We just keep doing what we're doing? Do you want a ceremony?"

Dover started to shake his head, then stopped. "Do *you* want a ceremony?"

Ben flushed and ran a hand over his loose, springy curls. "Yeah. I kinda do want a ceremony. It doesn't have to be big, but I'd like to celebrate. Fuck, I already have you a wedding present."

Dover sat up straight. "A present? I love presents."

Ben laughed. "Stay here a minute and I'll go get it." He groaned as he got out of bed and rolled his shoulders. "Damn, I ache. Will sex be like that every time?"

Dover set the breakfast tray on the floor and bounced in place on the bed. "Nope. Just when I'm in heat."

"You were in heat?" Ben's eyes widened. All omegas were fertile year-round, but once a year, they went into heat and were *extra* fertile.

Dover wrinkled his nose. "Don't look at me like that. It came early this year. Usually I stay home and play with my toys during my heat."

He hadn't wanted to get pregnant by accident like his brother Kit had. Pearl was adorable, but Dover didn't want to be a single parent.

Ben grinned. "Toys? Where are they at?"

Dover laughed. "I didn't have room in my bag for them and my heat wasn't supposed to happen for another three months." He pointed at the door. "Go get my present."

Ben chuckled, but obeyed.

Dover heard tiny paws and looked over the bed. "Hey, Jojo."

The puppy grinned at him, tongue hanging from her mouth. Dover picked her up and hugged her.

Ben came back into the room a few minutes later with a large driftwood-framed glass picture. He turned it around and Dover gasped, tears filling his eyes. "That's my waterfall!"

Small shards of glass in shades varying from white to dark blue were pieced together and smoothed to form his waterfall. Dark blue and green glass and stones formed the plunge pool and more of the creek. Ben had included green and brown foliage at the sides of the creek with colorful flowers dotted here and there. There was even the start of the stone staircase leading to the top of the cliff.

"Is that Chubber's stone?" Dover laughed. "Oh, there's Chubber!" Ben had placed Chubber's stone at the edge of the creek and a small brown glass otter sat on it.

Ben tapped the bottom of the picture. "What do you think of this?"

Dover wiped his eyes. At the bottom of the picture was a flower shaped like Dover's caudal fin. Within the center was his favorite pearl. "It's beautiful Ben. That's my waterfall."

Ben set the picture down and sat beside Dover,

pulling him into his arms. "Maybe one day we can go to the Silver Isles and see it together."

Dover buried his face against Ben's shoulder and let the tears fall. He missed home so much. It was more than just a pretty waterfall. It was his sanctuary. He could see Ben and him living there, raising a family, and loving on each other. That would never happen, though.

He swiped his eyes, then looked up. "Ben, I need to tell you something."

"What's wrong?" Ben stroked his back.

"My family really doesn't like humans. Well, my *father* really doesn't like humans."

"He's one person," Ben said, voice soothing. "We'll deal with it."

Dover groaned. "My father is the king of the Southern Silver Isles. I'm his youngest child."

Ben's hand froze and he choked on a cough. "Fuck! You're a prince?"

Dover sniffled and looked up. His mate looked horrified. "Yeah. My father decided it was time I married, but I had already started hearing the mating call. It led me here to you."

"He let you leave alone? Don't princes have to have bodyguards or something like that?" Ben's eyes darted around the room. "What if someone tries to kidnap and ransom you?"

Dover winced. "I didn't exactly tell anyone I was leaving. Except for Shauna and Nami of course."

Ben croaked out another cough. "We should call

him, right? To let him know you're okay. Fuck, he has to be worried."

"Ben, you're not hearing me," Dover said, sighing. "My father doesn't like humans. He wants me to marry some mer aristocrat. I told my mother about the mating call and she said to ignore it."

Ben's eyes narrowed and he growled. His arms tightened around Dover. "You're mine. They can't take you away."

Dover leaned back, sadness filling him. "I know you didn't ask for this, Ben. Life with you is easy, but if my family gets involved, it will definitely complicate things. I'm sure by now, my father knows I'm missing. We can never go back to the Silver Isles. He may even send people here if he finds me."

"Fuck."

Dover took a breath and closed his eyes. "If... if you don't want to be with me, I'll let you go."

Ben tipped his face up and kissed him. "No. We may have just met, but I know you, Dover. You're smart and beautiful. You make me feel like I'm really alive. Like I have a place in the world."

Dover's chest puffed out. His mate *liked* him.

"You're also a bit lazy, you snore, and you sing off-key while you cook. Your favorite speed is mosey, and you get excited over everything. You're territorial and sneaky, but your heart is the kindest I've ever seen."

Dover glared at Ben. "You should have stopped at me being smart and beautiful."

Ben laughed. "I love it all, Dover. I love you."

Dover smiled wide, happiness filling him. "Even

though I didn't tell you about my family before mating with you because I'm a selfish twat?"

"Even though you're a selfish twat who didn't tell me he's a prince," Ben said, chuckling. "I'm selfish too, Dover. I want you with me and I don't care what anyone else thinks."

Ben kissed him and Dover melted against him. Damn, his mate tasted good.

Dover leaned back, breaking the kiss. "Don't distract me. You have today off, so we need to go swimming."

Ben grunted and fell back on the bed. "Can't we just sleep in? You broke me last night."

Dover pulled Ben's toe. "Nope. You don't want to be *lazy*, do you?"

Ben laughed and rolled out of bed. "Okay, okay. I'll get Otis ready."

Dover leaned over and picked up the puppy. "Jojo needs swimming lessons too, don't you baby girl?"

A little while later, he settled a towel and cooler on the sand in front Ben's house. Dover liked that the ocean was right there. He missed his creek, but this spot wasn't so bad. Saltwater just had an odd taste to him.

Chubber scampered toward the water. He preferred freshwater too, but he had adapted as well as could be expected. The large freshwater fountain helped.

Ben is worth swimming in salty-tasting water, Dover thought. He cherished their swims. Ben was very capable in the water. For a human.

"Does Jojo really need this?" Ben asked, holding the puppy up. Jojo wore a bright pink puppy lifejacket.

Dover nodded and pulled his sarong off. "Until she gets bigger. Race me!"

Ben laughed and ran after him, Jojo in his arms and Otis following.

Dover called his tail as soon as the water was deep enough and took off with a large splash. He was familiar with the layout of Ben's beach now, so he knew right where the best kelp beds were and he wanted some more clams.

Splashing at the surface of the water made him look up and he grinned at Otis. The dog was his swimming buddy. Chubber swam circles around the big dog as he paddled after Dover. Ben brought up the rear, somehow managing to swim smoothly while pulling Jojo behind him.

Dover maybe missed his creek, but he had found something so much better.

CHAPTER 9

ONE MONTH LATER

*B*en walked down the beach toward the marina with Dover's hand in his. Chubber babbled at them from Ben's shoulder. The otter had a fancy seashell and pearl crown around his plump waist. Dover hadn't seemed all that concerned, so Ben had let Chubber keep it on.

Otis and Jojo ran in front of them, barking at birds and sniffing every bit of driftwood they came across. Ben bent and took a nice-looking piece from Otis and stuck it in the bag on his back. "Good boy."

"Otis is the best boy," Dover said, cooing. "I can't wait to see what's down there. Do you think I'll find pirate's treasure? Maybe it'll be all shiny and you can put it in your next piece."

Ben shook his head and smiled. It was too cold for a swim now, at least for Ben, but Dover had found a ship wreck off the coast and was determined to explore it while Ben fished.

"If you find treasure, we should sell it and buy you a

truck. It's getting cooler and you'll get pneumonia or something riding the Vespa everywhere."

Dover stuck his tongue out. "No! Velma is my one true love."

Ben arched a brow. "What am I then?"

Dover shrugged. "My other one true love. I'm a fickle man."

Ben laughed, then bent to take a stick from Jojo. "Thanks, sweet girl. You're just like Otis, aren't you?" The puppy was getting bigger, but she was still very much a puppy.

"Jojo is the bestest girl," Dover said, then smiled smugly. "Eloise couldn't believe I passed the driving test. She didn't want to give up Velma, but she promised."

"Now, she'll try to get you to work at the factory," Ben said with a laugh. He had been surprised Dover had passed too.

Dover shook his head. "Nope. I'm gonna be a treasure hunter. I'll make us rich."

Hester stood on her porch as they walked past her house. Her shoulders were wrapped in an old knitted shawl and her face looked grave. A small bag sat at her feet. "Ben, carry my bag. I'm going with you two today."

Ben shared a look with Dover. He didn't like the sound of that.

"Do we need to stay home?" Dover asked.

"No," she said firmly. "This needs to happen, but I want to be there if you need me. I won't have my scrying bowl, but I know a few tricks."

Ben fought the urge to turn around. He just wanted to spend the day with Dover. "We should go home."

Hester patted his cheek. "Get my bag, Ben. This needs to happen."

Dover's eyes were wide with excitement. "Am I going to discover a chest of gold and have to fight my way through a mob of ghost pirates?"

Ben groaned and looked up at the sky. "Why did I let him watch *Pirates of the Caribbean*? Why?"

Hester chuckled and patted Otis' head. "You're lucky to have him, Benny, and you know it. Come on. You need to get to catching us dinner."

They walked the rest of the way to the marina, and Ben just shook his head when he saw Eloise waiting at his dock. "Did Hester call you, or are you here to try to talk Dover into another job?"

Eloise snorted and pushed her sunglasses on top of her head. "Bluetail called me and asked if I wanted to come along."

Ben raised his brow and looked at Dover.

The merman gave him a sheepish look. "I thought we might need her help carrying all the treasure I'm going to find back to the house."

Eloise snorted and slapped Ben's back. "I'll help you catch some redfish, then we can make Dover cook them when he doesn't find his pirate treasure."

Dover shoved Eloise and the two started slapping at each other.

Ben sighed and helped Hester onto his boat, then tucked their gear in the tiny cabin.

Hester and Dover put lifejackets on Otis and Jojo

while Eloise maneuvered Ben's boat from the dock and sailed away from the marina.

Ben lay back in the bench seat and let Chubber climb onto his stomach. The little otter shimmied and danced, making him laugh.

Eloise shot him a grin. "It's nice to hear you laugh. We've been friends for a while, but you were always so reserved. Now that you have Dover, you laugh and smile and talk."

Ben shrugged and rubbed a finger over one of the pearls on the crown around Chubber's waist. "Dover makes life better. He *likes* being around me, Eloise. When we aren't together he actually misses me."

She frowned. "Are you thinking about your family?"

He nodded. "All my life, I've been a person's background. Does that make sense?"

Eloise gave him a puzzled look. "No."

"I've been there, but in the background," he tried to explain. "No one really noticed if I was there or not. I was just someone they knew."

Eloise growled and shook her head, making her brown curls bounce. "I would notice if you were gone. You're my best friend, Ben."

He grinned. "Yeah. You and Hester were the first to see me. Ryan, Stewart, and a few others at work notice me too, but all of you could live without me."

"You sound like a drama queen," Eloise said, rolling her eyes.

"I feel like a drama queen," he said, laughing. "At least where Dover's concerned. He would be upset without me, Eloise. He would grieve."

"I get what you're saying," Eloise said, "But I would grieve for you too. You're more loved than you think, douchebag."

Chubber braced his paws on Ben's cheeks and nibbled at his nose.

"Yeah, I feel loved." Ben watched Dover dance with Otis and Jojo at the front of the boat while Hester clapped. "I love him, Eloise."

She pushed her sunglasses over her eyes and smirked. "I kinda noticed."

"Ben," Dover said, running into the cabin. "Come listen to the waves with me. It's the most beautiful song."

Ben set Chubber on Eloise's head and went to stand with his mate. He wrapped his arms around Dover and listened to him chatter about the wreck.

An hour later, Dover told them to stop and shucked his pants. He jumped into the ocean, legs shifting to his silvery blue tail. "You all follow me and I'll show you where to stop, okay?"

"Got it, bluetail," Eloise said, leaning over the rail. "If I run over you, I apologize in advance. You kinda blend into the water."

Dover splashed water with his tail, drenching Eloise. "Don't let the hairy beaver run over me, Ben."

Ben sighed. "And... the beaver jokes begin."

"I'm too busy looking for hard wood to hear you, bluetail," Eloise said, cackling. She moved back to the cabin.

"Wood? Did you switch teams, Eloise?" Hester

asked, sitting down on the bench in the cabin, Jojo in her arms. "I thought you liked over wet beavers."

Ben gagged, keeping a careful hold on Chubber. "Come on, buddy. It's getting gross over there."

Eloise and Hester laughed at him, but he ignored them and went to the front of the boat.

Ben leaned over the rail and watched Dover swim just below the surface. His tail was one big muscle, and he moved almost as fast as the boat. "I wish I could swim with you."

Dover gurgled something and Ben shook his head. "I don't understand your bubble language," Ben yelled, not sure if Dover could hear him underwater.

"I need to learn it," Eloise said from the cabin. "Not that I'll ever meet other merfolk, but it has to suck to not be able to speak your native language to anyone but an otter."

"I would learn it if I could," Ben said, sulking. He hated the thought of not being everything Dover needed. Otis sat beside him and leaned against his leg.

About thirty minutes later, Dover told them to stop. "It's right here. I'll swim down and look around, then be right back. Wait to start fishing until I get the layout figured out."

"Be careful," Ben said. The boat rocked as they dropped anchor. The water wasn't rough by any means, but it was a small boat and they were in open ocean. "I should suit up and go with him."

Eloise came to stand beside him. "You'd distract him. Let him have his look, then you can suit up and I'll shift. My beaver hates saltwater, but I'll do some dives

87

and try to keep an eye on him. How far down is the wreck?"

"About two hundred and twenty feet," Ben said.

"You don't have the right equipment, so neither of us can go that deep. I can still try to check on him." Eloise started pulling her shirt up.

"Keep your clothes on, beaver," Hester said. "We need to stay on the boat."

"Why?" Eloise asked, looking at Hester over her shoulder.

Hester pointed at the water. "That's why."

Ben turned back to the water and his heart started pounding. "Fuck."

Seconds ago, the surface of the water had been empty, but now, Ben counted at least twelve dorsal fins sticking out of the water and circling the boat.

"Sharks," Eloise said, voice shaking.

CHAPTER 10

*D*over swam around the sunken ship, admiring the corals and beautiful flytrap anemones growing along the wreck. The water was much cooler in the ocean depths, and it had a very different feel than the shallow waters he was used to. *Adventure, thy name is Dover!*

The backside of the ship was buried in the sand, but the front half of the ship was visible. The wooden hull looked ancient, but Dover wasn't an expert.

"Damn," he said. "Pirates didn't have metal ships."

A line of empty window frames covered one side of the wreckage. He swam inside and looked around. All he saw was rotting wood, kelp, and coral growths. Small fish darted around, and Dover took a moment to appreciate the life around him. Merfolk needed land, but they also needed water.

"I should spend more time in the ocean," he said.

"That would be a bad idea, little guppy." The deep voice startled him, and he turned around quickly.

A large merman was silhouetted in the window. His dark hair was cut close to his head, and his dark eyes glittered in the very faint light. The man wore slick black armor and the handle of a harpoon gun poked over his shoulder. Small blades were strapped to his chest and arms.

He swam into the room and Dover's eyes widened further. He was a shark-tailed merman. A *Great White* shark-tailed merman. *Eep!*

Dover noted the man wore thin black gloves and narrowed his eyes, searching his memory. "You look familiar."

The merman bowed slightly. "Prince Tack of the Northern Silver Isles, at your service, Your Highness."

Dover grinned and breathed out bubbles of relief. "Shew! I thought you were some renegade mer out to murder innocent treasure hunters."

Tack raised a brow. "Treasure hunters?"

Dover waved his arms around the empty room. "I'm searching for treasure."

"I'm afraid we already processed the visible portion of this wreck," Tack said. "We're scheduled to excavate the bottom half next week."

Dover's shoulders slumped. "Oh. I didn't discover an unknown pirate wreck?"

Tack gave him a small smile. "No, I'm sorry, but this was actually an eighteenth century Spanish merchant's ship."

"Damn it! I don't want to work at the factory." Dover swished his tail angrily. "I forgot you Coalswells were divers. You probably find all the best ships."

"We do," Tack agreed, nodding. "Your father calls us scavengers."

Dover rolled his eyes. "Not everyone can be pearl farmers. No one else is better suited to underwater exploration."

"My kingdom does well," Tack said, and started slowly circling Dover. "We patrol the seas, looking for wreckage. That's how one of my men spotted you last week. Imagine my surprise when he told me King Ren's youngest son was swimming alone so very far from home."

"Shit a brick! You can't tell my father, okay?" Dover rubbed his face. "Please."

"My diplomat in your court, Janine, keeps up on all the gossip," Tack said, ignoring him. "Just last week, Prince Kai and Prince Kit went on a quick trip to the Bahamas with a couple of servants. The only thing is, my people saw your brothers swimming up the coast of Florida."

Dover frowned. "Why would they do that?"

Tack grinned, sharp teeth gleaming white in the shadows of the wreck. "Why would their servants take a ship to Virginia and start swimming down the coast?"

"Uh oh," Dover said, finally realizing what Tack was getting at. "They're looking for me."

"Yes," Tack said, tail swishing. "Without any guards or escorts."

"Why would father agree to that? Kai is second in line to inherit the throne."

"Prince Kai is more than capable of protecting himself, but your father is under the impression several guards went with him." Tack looked troubled. "Janine said that your father doesn't know you're missing."

Dover opened his mouth, then closed it. His father didn't know he was missing? How was that possible? "It's almost been two months.

"Janine told me your sister Eugenia is getting married, so the king's court has been busy," Tack said, wincing. "That must be why your disappearance has gone unnoticed."

"You don't have to lie to me," Dover whispered. "I bet your father would notice if you went missing."

"He would." Tack stopped circling him and rubbed his chin. "Your brothers noticed. They're looking for you. That's something at least."

"Yeah." Dover sighed again, then went rigid when he saw a large Great White shark swim past the ship's window. "Shit, watch out. There's a big shark outside. We better get back to the boat."

Tack looked over his shoulder. "She's with me. My people and our pets are all over this site, so it's safe enough for you right now."

Dover grinned. "Your pet is a shark?"

Tack grinned back. "Pet is probably the wrong word." He paused and tapped his ear. A small black metal strip was hooked around it. "My lookout tells me a human with a knife just jumped off your boat and is attempting to swim down."

Dover swam out the window and started for the surface. "That's my Ben. He must have seen your sharks and freaked out."

"Your Ben?" Tack kept pace with him easily. "My people will keep him from drowning."

Dover flushed. "Ben is my mate."

"You mated a human?" Tack sounded horrified. "The dumbass just jumped into an ocean full of sharks, so he can't be very intelligent. Are you sure he's your mate?"

Dover noticed several shark-tailed merfolk and large sharks swimming around the wreckage. Most of the Coalswells were shark tailed, but he had never seen so many in one place before. "He's all mine. You really have a shark friend?"

Tack nodded to Dover's other side and Dover jumped. The Great White was *right beside him*. "That's Lola. She's my friend. Don't worry. She won't eat you as long as you're with me."

"What if I meet her and you're not there?"

"Then you're dinner." Tack grinned. "There's a reason guppy tails don't swim alone in the ocean."

Dover caught sight of his mate, thrashing around in the water. Two mermen held him by the arms. "My poor Ben was probably worried about me."

Tack gave him a flat look. "He jumped into shark-infested water. Should he really reproduce?"

Two large splashes came from the right and Dover covered his cheeks with his hand. "This is so embarrassing, but that's my friend Eloise and our dog Otis. Oh, and there's my Chubber."

Chubber swam with quick precision, and put his small body between Lola and Dover.

Tack grinned. "Brave little otter."

A beaver swam right toward Tack's face and Dover did his best not to laugh as the prince fought to hold her away from him.

"Eloise, it's okay." Dover sighed, and hugged Eloise, pulling her away from Tack. "I wish she understood me." The beaver went slack and looked at him, trying to see through the murky water.

"Let's get to the surface before anyone else jumps from your boat and attacks me," Tack said, scowling.

They broke surface and Dover immediately searched for Ben and Otis. Both were being held afloat by mermen.

"Dover!" Ben stopped struggling against the mermen. "Damn it, bluetail. There are sharks everywhere."

"This is your human?" Tack asked, clearly unimpressed.

Dover hummed in pleasure. "Yes, isn't he beautiful?"

"He almost stabbed me in the eye," the merman on Ben's left said sourly.

Dover eyed Tack's look of disdain, then started giggling. "Your prince took a wet beaver to the face."

Eloise growled and all of Tack's guards started laughing.

Tack gave him an annoyed look. "Thank you, Prince Dover, for telling everyone about that."

"Dover, what's going on?" Ben watched them all warily.

"To be honest, I don't know. Let's get on the boat," Dover said.

A merman approached from the other side of the

boat. "Um, Your Highness? There's a witch onboard and she turned three of our men into raccoons."

Tack blinked. "Like, *actual* raccoons?"

Another merman swam over. He held a wet raccoon out of the water. "Your Highness? What should we do?"

"Hester," Dover yelled. "Stop turning them into raccoons."

"Loosen your panties, boys. It's only temporary." Hester looked over the rail, Jojo in her arms. "Has he tried to kidnap you yet, Dover?"

Dover gasped, finally understanding why the Coalswells had arrived when they did. "Prince Tack, are you trying to kidnap me?"

"I'll kill you, you son of a bitch!" Ben punched one of the mermen in the face, and bit the arm of the tiger-shark-tailed merman on his right. Freed, he swam to Dover.

Dover held him up in the water with one arm, Eloise in the other. His tail swished below, keeping them afloat.

Tack sighed. "I'm not going to kidnap you."

Dover smiled, relieved. "Oh good."

"I mean, I was, but honestly, your human's a handful." Tack grinned when both Eloise and Ben growled at him.

"I like their dog," the merman holding Otis said. He scratched behind Otis' ear. "You're a good boy, aren't you?"

"Woof." Otis' tongue hung out and he leaned into the man's scratches.

"Well, he doesn't bite," the tiger-shark-tailed merman said, glaring at Ben. "Unlike the human."

Tack's expression grew serious. "Really, though, you need to call your brothers and go home. It's not safe for you to be unprotected."

"I protect him," Ben said, snarling.

Tack arched a brow. "You're one man, human. I had intended to take him and ransom him to his father. I could still do that and there is nothing you could do to stop me."

Hester snapped her fingers and another merman turned into a raccoon. "Would you like to repeat that, Your Highness? Ben *isn't* alone."

The mermaid next to the scrambling raccoon grabbed him from the water with a wince.

"Why aren't you kidnapping him?" Ben asked, eyes hard.

"He's mated to a human," Tack said, smirking. "I feel sorry for the man."

"My human is perfect," Dover said, growling.

"If you say so," Tack said, shrugging. "Your father won't be happy. If you happen to need protection, the Northern Silver Isles will take you and your mate in."

Dover's mouth dropped open. The Coalswells were supposed to be cruel and evil. "Why would you do that?"

Tack grinned. "It would make King Ren furious."

"Ah," Dover said, understanding. "What do you want from my father?"

"There will be a union between our families," Tack

said. "I need to be able to choose which of your siblings I marry."

"Talia will kick your ass," Dover said.

"I don't want to marry Princess Talia," Tack said, face bland. "Get on your boat and go home. Call your brothers."

Dover swam around Lola and went to the rear of the boat so Ben and Eloise could board. Chubber climbed Dover's body to jump onto the boat and Otis doggy-paddled over so Dover could help him clamber onto the stern. By the time he shifted and pulled himself out of the water, the Coalswells were gone.

CHAPTER 11

*B*en hugged Dover to him the entire way home. "Never again. You can never go swimming alone again."

Dover kissed his chin. "I wasn't expecting that. Did you see all those sharks?"

"I almost pissed myself when I jumped in," Ben said, shuddering. He had recognized the Great Whites, Tigers, and Hammerheads, but there had been more than he could count.

"That was stupid," Eloise said, wincing. "You just had a knife, Ben."

"You're a beaver," Ben said, glaring at his friend. "You shouldn't have been jumping in the ocean either."

Eloise gave him an innocent look and steered the boat. "I was just following Otis."

"It doesn't matter now," Hester said. "It went well, and I'm glad you got to meet the northern prince."

"What have you seen, Hester?" Dover leaned toward her, but his hands stayed bunched in Ben's shirt.

"I've seen many things, but also a lot of nothing," Hester said, sighing. "Foretelling a person's future isn't easy, you know. Most of the time I'm guessing based on bits and pieces I've seen. You and Ben just need to keep doing what you're doing. You two have an important role in preserving the Silver Isles."

"That isn't very helpful," Dover said, wrinkling his nose. "Should I call Kai and Kit?"

"I'm not a magic eight-ball, Dover," Hester said, frowning. "Do what you think is right."

"I think you should," Ben said, sighing. "Prince Tack intended to kidnap you, Dover. What if someone else shows up? I want to protect you, but I'm just one person."

"It's not safe for them to be swimming up and down the coast," Dover said, shuddering. "Those sharks were huge. Kai can handle himself, but Kit isn't allowed around sharp objects."

Ben arched a brow. "Why?"

Dover grinned. "He's a bit clumsy. After he accidently cut the tip of Lord Gianni's tail off, Father and Mother forbade him from training with the guards, like Kai."

Eloise laughed. "Please tell me Lord Gianni deserved it. Please."

Dover made a face. "He so deserved it. A lot of the lords in Father's court deserve it."

Ben buried his face in Dover's hair and ignored them as they talked about Dover's two brothers. Apparently, Kai and Kit were the only siblings Dover had a relationship with.

Ben knew changes were coming. If Prince Tack hadn't felt sorry for Dover, he would have taken him and killed everyone else. There hadn't been anything Ben could do. He didn't like feeling helpless. He had to bring Dover back to the Silver Isles.

When they reached the marina, Ben handed Dover his cell phone. "Call your brothers. Give them our address."

Dover bit his lip. "I won't leave you, Ben. You promised I could stay with you forever."

Ben cupped his face and gave him a gentle kiss. "You can stay with me forever, Dover, but we'll be living in safety in the Silver Isles."

"What?" Eloise leaned over Dover's shoulder and glared at Ben. "You're leaving me?"

"Dover can't be kidnapped in the Silver Isles," Ben said. "There are guards and other merfolk all over the place. I can't lose him, Eloise."

She scowled. "Yeah. I get it. I don't like it, but I get it. I about had a heart attack when you told me he was a prince."

Hester smiled, eyes dancing. "Better make that call, Dover."

"If they're swimming, he won't be able to answer right away." Dover groaned, then dialed a number and held the phone to his ear. After a few seconds, he left a message. "Hey, Kai. This is Dover. Prince Tack said you and Kit were looking for me. I'll text you our address."

Dover hung up and buried his face against Ben's chest. "Promise you won't leave me, Ben. No matter how annoying my family gets."

Ben kissed the top of his head. "I promise."

Eloise bounced on the balls of her feet. "I'll stay with you two. If the fuckers try to take him, Ben, I'll maul them."

"Death by beaver," Hester said, chuckling. "What a way to go. Eloise, take Dover to the car. Ben and I will unload."

Ben quickly packed up the cooler and snacks. Once Dover and Eloise were far enough away, he turned to Hester. "What's going on?"

She watched him for a moment, eyes dark and serious. "Since the beginning of history, humans have feared the other species. Shifters, merfolk, witches, vampires, elves, and all the other species have skills that humans don't have."

"Is this supposed to make me feel better?" Ben asked, irritated. "I know humans are the weakest species. I fought beside shifters and vampires in the marines. I know I'm at a disadvantage here."

"You have something that no other being in this world has," Hester said.

"What's that?" Ben asked. He knew he was a good shot and excellent at hand to hand, but he sure as shit couldn't breathe under water.

"You have Dover's love," Hester said. "You have his loyalty and his adoration."

Ben's laugh was rough even to his own ears. "How does that protect him?"

Hester's smile was full of something Ben didn't recognize. He would almost call it awe. "It will protect more than just him. Trust in yourself, Ben. I can't see all the future holds, but I know that you are perfectly capable of being exactly what Dover needs."

Ben groaned. "Hedge witches suck ass."

"Only when we're asked nicely," Hester laughed. "Get the bags and move it, handsome."

LATE THAT NIGHT, Ben and Dover sat around a small fire on the beach in front of his house. Eloise had called in reinforcements, so half the restaurant staff had arrived an hour ago.

Stewart leaned back in his chair, a bat lying across his lap. Ryan was shifted and circled Ben and Dover with Otis, growling at every little crack of the fire. Ryan's sister, Alicia, and her mate Dahlia had left their newborn at home. They sat with several others from the local wolf shifter pack.

"You have a lot of friends," Dover whispered, leaning his head on Ben's shoulder. Ben was happy to have his mate in his lap. It made it easier to hold him.

"I didn't realize." Ben met Hester's gaze across the fire. "I should have."

"Are you sure you want to leave here, Ben? We can find a way to stay."

Ben stroked Dover's bare back. "I like it here, Dover, but you're my home. As long as I'm with you, it doesn't matter where we are."

"Ben," Dover said, eyes wide. "I love you."

"Sweet," Eloise said, kneeling beside them. "Enough with the mush. What's our game plan here? We have wolves, humans, and me, the greatest beaver in all the land. Do you think there will be a fight?"

"Not with my brothers," Dover said, laughing. "They're good people. I promise."

"What the fuck is that?" one of the wolves asked, standing up and instantly shifting.

A large saltwater crocodile walked from the waves, the fire glinting off his eyes and a slender figure at his side.

Dover sat up, his expression morphing from worry to pure joy. "That's Romeu and Nami!"

He jumped from Ben and started running. The mermaid squealed and ran for him too.

Ben stood, eyes were on the crocodile. It was huge and those teeth were sharp. Ryan growled and came to stand at his side. Otis growled from Ben's other side and Ryan paused to glare at the dog.

"Ryan, behave. You both are fierce, protective good boys," Ben said, fighting a smile.

Dover and Nami had reached each other and were hugging and bouncing around.

The crocodile ignored them and headed for the fire. It was at least twenty-five feet long, tail to snout. As one, Ben's friends stood up and glared at the crocodile. Shifted wolves started circling the beast. Stewart stood on his chair and waved his bat.

"Romeu, be nice," Dover called over his shoulder.

"Jojo," Eloise called out, scrambling to keep ahold of the puppy. Jojo hit the ground running, tongue hanging out and tail wagging. She dodged wolves and grabbing hands and ran straight for the crocodile.

"Jojo, no," Ben called out, scrambling to intercept her. He didn't reach her in time.

The crocodile froze when the puppy hopped around him and started licking his snout. Any lingering fear Ben held disappeared when the crocodile dropped to the ground and let the puppy crawl onto his back.

"Fuck." Ben noted Hester's grin and cleared his throat, approaching the shifter at a more sedate pace. "So... Romeu is it? This is Jojo – your new puppy."

The crocodile shifted and seconds later a naked man stood in its place, holding Jojo in his arms. "Seriously?" He lifted the puppy up and laughed when Jojo licked his face. "Who's a good girl? You are, yes you are. My wife is going to kill me."

"Ben," Dover called out, dragging his friend behind him. "Nami, this is my Ben. Isn't he beautiful?"

The small woman had a pointed chin and short dark hair framing her heart-shaped face. Her long-sleeved swim shirt had a large cat-mermaid on it, and she had a waterproof pack strapped to her back.

The woman's dark eyes looked him up and down. "He's alright, I guess."

"Nami," Dover said, gasping. "Look at his shoulders and his perfect face. Do you even see his eyes? What about his lips?" He leaned up and kissed Ben. "I love his lips."

Nami wrinkled her nose. "Yeah, no thanks."

Eloise sauntered over. "Hey there, lovely. How do you feel about a wet, hot beaver?"

Nami smirked. "Depends how she tastes."

"Ew, ew, ew," Dover said, burying his face against Ben's chest. "It's not funny when I can visualize her puns. Where's the bleach? I need to clean my brain."

Hester cackled. "You'll have to get used to it."

Ben tilted his head and eyed Eloise. His friend was flushed and trembly, her eyes full of hope. He knew exactly what she was feeling. *She's found her mate.*

"Dover?" The voice came from the waves. Two men waded from the water. They wore slick, long-sleeved swim shirts and sarongs.

"The brunette is Kai and the redhead is Kit," Dover whispered to Ben. "No matter what, remember I love you."

Ben ignored the approaching men and kissed Dover, savoring his taste and the feel of his mate pressed against his body.

"Who the hell are you?" The brunette asked, practically vibrating with anger. Kai was large, with broad shoulders and a blunt, square jaw.

Dover hummed, looking a little dazed. "Kai, this is my mate, Ben."

The redhead covered his mouth and squealed in glee before he started bouncing. Kit wasn't at all what Ben had expected. The redhead was plump, with a round face covered with freckles.

"You found your mate? Is that why you were so mopey before you left? You were hearing the mating call." Kit pulled his brother into his arms and hugged him. "I'm so happy for you. Now you won't be all alone in your cottage and you'll smile all the time."

Eloise snorted. "He doesn't smile when Ben makes him clean up all the sand he brings in from the beach."

Nami gasped dramatically and placed her hand on Dover's forehead. "You cleaned something? Are you sick, your highness?"

Ben choked off his laugh and tried to look innocent when Dover glared at him.

"You're mated?" Kai looked conflicted. "I don't know if I should hug you or swear. This complicates things, Dover."

"Prince Kai," Alicia said, coming to stand beside Ben. "Come sit by the fire and explain how much trouble our Ben is in. He's a good man and Dover loves him very much."

Kai gave a half-hearted smile. "You're the alpha of all these wolves?"

Alicia nodded. "I'm Alpha Alicia."

Kai bowed. "It's a pleasure to meet you. I apologize for my rudeness."

Alicia grinned. "Not a problem. You're worried about your brother."

Ben kept a firm hold on Dover as they moved to the fire. His omega gave him a reassuring smile and squeezed his hand. "Romeu is a nice guy, so Jojo will have a good home."

Ben watched the crocodile shifter wrap a towel around his waist while keeping a hold on the wiggling puppy. He grunted. "Sure."

Kai sat down and eyed Ben and Dover. "Father doesn't know you're missing. Kit went to visit you two days after you left but couldn't find you. He got me and we searched everywhere. Nami and Shauna wouldn't tell us anything except that you were safe."

"We told Talia and she said to give you some time," Kit said. "Once your month was up, we thought Father would discover you were gone, but Eugenia got engaged to Lord Eades' son, so everyone got distracted."

Nami winced. "By then, we didn't know where you were. George wouldn't tell us a thing. He said you found your mate and we should leave you alone."

Kai scowled. "He's an annoying beaver."

"I love George," Dover said, leaning against Ben. "He's the best beaver ever. Except for Eloise because she gave me Velma."

Kit pursed his lips. "Velma?"

"My Vespa." Dover preened. "It has a sidecar. I'll give you a ride tomorrow."

Kit bounced in his seat. "That sounds fun."

"Anyway," Kai said, giving his brothers a hard look. "Talia sent us to find you. We knew you headed to the United States, so Nami and your friend Romeu took the north and Kit and I took the south. None of the merfolk we came across knew where you were."

Dover shrugged. "I haven't seen any merfolk until today. Prince Tack showed up at a shipwreck I was looking through."

Kai growled and jumped to his feet. "Did the fucker hurt you? I'll tear the filthy scavenger to pieces."

Kit's eyes were wide. "I hear he has a pet shark and feeds it any merfolk that annoy him."

Eloise laughed. "I attacked him and all he did was glare. He's good people."

Dover smiled. "He and his people were very nice. He was actually the one that told me to call you."

"Prince Tack was nice?" Kit asked in disbelief. "Seriously?"

"He must want something," Kai said, scowling. "The Coalswells are nothing but trouble."

Hester snorted. "Look a little closer to home for enemies, tiger prince."

"What do you see?" Ben asked, eying his friend.

"King Ren's court is full of vipers," Hester said. "Soon enough there will be a clash between the young and the old."

"The curse," Dover whispered, swallowing.

"What curse?" Alicia leaned forward, eyes concerned.

"Oh, my god," Dahlia said, covering her mouth. "Do you mean the Sea Witch's curse is real? My mother used to tell me the story when I was a little girl."

They all turned to Hester, and the woman shrugged. "Ask the princes. They should be more familiar with it than I am."

CHAPTER 12

*D*over buried his face against Ben's neck and breathed deeply. His mate's smell always soothed him. The Sea Witch's curse had always seemed half fairy tale, half historical event to him. Now it was too real. He shuddered and Ben's arms tightened around him.

Chubber ran across the sand and climbed into his lap, rubbing his head against Dover's chin. Dover hugged him and leaned back.

Kai cleared his throat. Six generations ago, the three kingdoms of The Silver Isles were completely at peace."

"The three kingdoms," Stewart said, confused. "I thought it was just The Northern Silver Isles and the Southern Silver Isles."

"That's all you can see now," Kit said, shrugging. "Back then, there was also The Kingdom of the Deep. It was a large city above a deep trench that split the Northern and Southern kingdoms."

"The Northern and Southern kingdoms were led

by kings and the Kingdom of the Deep was led by the Sea Witch," Dover said, breathing in Ben's scent again. "The Northern Silver Isles kept mostly to itself, but the people of The Deep and The Southern Silver Isles mixed together through matings and friendship. In fact, the Southern king was the Sea Witch's brother."

"The Sea Witch," Alicia whispered. "They sound ominous."

"She was just a woman," Hester said sadly. "All witches are told the story of the most powerful witch in the world and the two men that broke her."

"She held all the power of the oceans," Kit said quietly. "She could use it to destroy a kingdom in an instance."

"She could also heal the waters around her from all pollution and corruption," Hester said firmly. "Her primary duty, however, was protection."

Dover frowned. He had never heard that before. What would the Sea Witch protect? Each of the kingdoms protected themselves.

"Like I said," Kai said, "The three kingdoms lived in peace until the two kings made a very foolish pact. They wanted the rich and beautiful Kingdom of the Deep."

"You said the Southern king was her brother," Alicia said, eyes watering. Ryan went to her side and she wrapped her arms around him. "Family is everything."

Kit plopped against Dover and Ben, hugging them both. "Family *is* everything."

Dover's lip trembled and he hugged his brother. It

had hurt to think that his family hadn't noticed he was gone. He should have had more faith in Kit and Kai.

"The two kings made a plan to overthrow her," Kai continued. "The Southern king was her trusted family and was welcome in her kingdom at any time. The Northern king was welcomed for an entirely different reason."

"He was her fated mate," Dover said, voice breaking. "I could never imagine betraying Ben. I don't understand what the man was thinking."

"He was a greedy, son of a bitch," Hester said, snarling. "He used the mating call to beguile her. He seduced her, then betrayed her."

"The two kings isolated the Sea Witch from her guards," Kai said, swallowing. "Then, together, they murdered her."

"Those fuckers," Stewart said, stroking his bat. "Please tell me they didn't get away with it."

"They didn't," Kai said. "Before she died, the Sea Witch cursed both men. Any mer of her brother's bloodline that ruled the Southern Silver Isles would always know strife within his family. He would always die by his child's hand. That was six generations ago."

"It happens every time," Kit said. "The first king was murdered by his son so that he could take the throne early. The next tried to murder his own child but was killed instead. Our grandfather went mad. He began to kill all the guppy tailed merfolk. He said he was purging the Silver Isles."

"Our father had to kill him," Kai said. "For our kingdom's sake."

"Ervin told me Father and Grandfather were very close to one another," Dover said. "Everyone thought they would break the curse because they loved one another so much."

"Hester," Ben said. "Are you saying the curse is about to come into play again?"

"Yes," Hester said. She looked at Kai, Kit, and Dover. "Your kingdom is a powder keg just waiting to be lit."

"Father wouldn't hurt us," Kit said, voice uncertain. "Would he?"

"He purposely had as many children as possible so he would have several heirs and he keeps an emotional distance from us," Kai said bitterly. "No one truly knows his heart, Kit."

"What about the Northern king?" Dahlia asked. "Was he cursed too?"

"Yes," Dover said. "He betrayed his mate, so the Sea Witch's curse ensured that while the king's descendants would hear the mating call, their mates would not. They would have to woo their mates and convince them to stay with them without the mating call's influence."

"That doesn't seem that bad," Stewart said. "Humans don't always hear a mating call, and we still fall in love."

"The curse also ensures that their touch would be painful to any living creature but their mate," Hester said, "and until their mate falls in love with them, the mer's touch would also be painful for them."

"So they can't have sex with anyone but their mate and only if they can convince their mate to love them?" Dahlia asked.

"Yes." Hester looked sad. "She wanted to make them work for their happiness. So far, it hasn't happened. The Northern kings aren't exactly known for their charm."

"The first king only managed to produce heirs by force," Kit said, shuddering. "It's said he killed thirteen omegas while trying to get them to conceive."

"One managed to survive," Ben said. "Prince Tack and his father are proof enough of that."

"Yes," Dover said. "The last few generations used artificial insemination. None have mated or even married."

"Yet Prince Tack wishes to marry one of King Ren's children," Hester said, a small smile on her face. "Hmm."

"What happened to the Kingdom of the Deep?" Eloise asked. "I've never heard of it."

"No one really knows," Dover said. "They live in the trench now. There is no beautiful city."

Hester snorted. "When the Sea Witch died, she transferred her power to her apprentice. The poor boy wasn't ready, and the transference caused the city to sink into the trench. Her people lived, but their city is far from sight now."

"How do you know all that?" Kai asked.

Hester sighed. "The Witches Council uses the Sea Witch's story as a lesson in caution. The Sea Witch has a great deal of power, but the title also comes with an important responsibility."

"There's still a Sea Witch?" Stewart asked, frowning.

"Yes," Hester said. "As long as the world exists, there

will be a Sea Witch. Now, it's time to get to bed. I called George and he'll be here with his ship tomorrow morning. Ryan and Stewart will pack your belongings and we'll get them to you as soon as possible."

Dover was almost ashamed of the excitement that filled him. He loved Ben so much, but he missed home. Now, he would have Ben *and* his cottage. His father couldn't make him marry anyone now.

He placed a hand on his flat abdomen and kissed Ben's shoulder. *It's too late to marry me off.*

"Tomorrow? You can't leave so soon," Eloise said, eyes on Nami.

Nami looked so sad. "I have to go. Dover needs me."

"Ben needs Eloise too," Dover said quickly. "She's his best friend, so she should come with us. Right, Eloise? For Ben."

Eloise's eyes never left Nami's face. "Yeah. For Ben. I'm going to go pack my shit."

"Yes," Romeu said, cheering. "I won't be the only shifter in our lake."

Ben looked at Dover. "I'm feeling used."

Dover leaned up and bit his chin. "Shush. I'll make it up to you tonight.

"Okay," Alicia said, clapping her hands. "Pack, let's help our friends. Diego, Selena, and Matt will go get boxes and packing paper. Ryan and Dahlia will go get our trucks. We'll have Ben and his mate ready to go by morning. Get moving!"

Alicia and her wolves got to work and packed everything in the house. Dover just watched in awe as the wolves efficiently fetched boxes, labeled them, then carefully packed Ben's art pieces, Dover's shinies, and everything else.

"Holy shit, Alicia," Ben said. Otis woofed softly, watching closely as someone bagged up his chew toys. Chubber and Nami wandered the house collecting all the otter's treasures. He had stashed them everywhere.

"No sense in having to wait for your things," the alpha said, nodding. "You should call Stephanie and let her know you won't be back to work at the restaurant. She'll hate to lose you, but she'll understand. I can help you sell the beach house too if you want."

Ben looked around. "I'm going to rent it to Ryan. He can stay here in exchange for maintaining the place."

Alicia smiled softly. "You're a good man, Ben."

Romeu tugged Dover away from Ben. "Dover, are you sure this is a good idea? I don't think Lord Eades is going to like you mating with someone. Shauna said he had plans for you." He gently cupped Dover's abdomen. "You smell different, you know. Maybe you should stay here with your mate. It would be safer."

Dover bit his lip. "That was the plan, but the Coalswells found me. That means that any of Father's enemies can."

Romeu looked nervous and danced from foot to foot, hugging Jojo to him. "Your father's enemies are on the island, Dover."

Dover frowned. "What do you mean?"

"You know Joy works in the castle, right?"

Dover nodded. Joy was a guppy tail and Romeu's wife.

"She cleans Lady Eades' room and she's heard a lot of things. People don't see the servants."

"What are you saying, Romeu?"

"Lord and Lady Eades hate your parents. Now, their son is marrying one of King's Ren's daughters. That puts him in line for the throne."

Dover gasped. "We have to tell Father."

Romeu rolled his eyes. "Would he believe our half-assed theories over his dear friend, Lord Eades?"

Dover sniffed, eyes watering. "No. He wouldn't."

"I told your brother," Romeu said, nodding at Kai. "He told Princess Talia. Maybe your father will listen to her."

Dover rubbed his face. "This is why I wanted to stay here with Ben forever. My family complicates everything."

Warm hands massaged his shoulders and a familiar scent soothed him. "Don't worry, love. I have your back. We'll figure this mess out."

"You have me too," Romeu said, nodding. "You know all the guppy tails love you. You think being called the guppy prince is an insult, but they see it as a compliment. You're their voice."

"I'm not much of a voice," Dover said, feeling guilty.

"You will be," Kai said from behind him. "Romeu is right. You're in the position to truly represent our people. Maybe it's time to step up."

Dover looked at Ben. The way his mate watched him made Dover think maybe he could do more for the guppy tails. Maybe he could be a real prince.

Dover looked up and smiled. "Okay. Let's go home."

CHAPTER 13

A week later, Ben held Otis' leash in his hand and leaned against the rail of the ship. George had appeared as promised and Alicia and her pack had helped them load all of Ben's belongings, even his truck and motorcycle. He had a lot more to bring leaving Aunt Prue's beach house than when he arrived. He had a lot more friends to say goodbye too as well.

"I never thought I would say this about a witch," Dover said, leaning into his side, "but I miss Hester."

"Me too," Ben said, tightening his arm around Dover. "She promised to come to the wedding. Ryan and Stewart will try to come too."

Kit winced. The merman stood on Dover's other side. "I hope father lets you have a wedding."

"We'll have a fucking wedding," Dover said, growling. "My mate wants one so it *will* happen, even if it's only at my waterfall."

Ben grinned. His mate's growl was too cute to be

scary. Chubber sat in Dover's arms and hissed as he waved his paws. *My protectors*, Ben thought, chuckling.

Kit grinned. "Kai and I will stand with you, Dover. Plus, you have to put Pearl in the wedding. You know you're her favorite uncle."

"Fuck that," Kai muttered from beside Ben. "*I'm* the one that buys her anything she wants. I should be her favorite."

"I don't know," Romeu said from where he lounged in a chair on the deck of the ship. "Dover spends the most time with Pearl. You have your work cut out for you, Prince Kai."

Ben tuned out their bickering and watched Latch Bay approach. Small, green mountains dominated the inland isles and clouds circled the peaks. He knew from Dover's description that a large river cut through the entire isles and multiple lakes were nestled within the hills of the southern half.

The gleaming white castle stood out from the rest of the approaching city. After his time in the marines, he shouldn't be surprised that something so clean and beautiful could conceal deadly corruption. The city looked so nice, though.

Have to keep up appearances for the tourists, Ben thought, wanting to snarl.

The rest of the town spread out across the bay and carried over onto the water. Ships and submerged shuttles filled the waters of the bay.

"Holy shit," he said, leaning over the rail. A herd of hippocampi swam by, their heads rising above the water before diving below. "My god, I've never seen so many at once."

"That's just one herd," Kai said, smiling. "We have six herds that we track around our kingdom. One even lives in the largest lake. They're a protected species here."

"So are the sprites," Kit said, leaning around Dover. "We have water sprites all over the isles and forest sprites further inland. On the very top of the highest mountain, there are even a few air sprites."

"Sprites are extinct in North America," Ben said, voice full of wonder. "I saw a water sprite when I was deployed once." The small creature had been made completely of water, but was humanoid in shape. It had been beautiful.

"There's a few in my creek," Dover said, leaning up to kiss him. "I'll introduce you, but they usually keep to themselves."

"They make their homes in the less populated places in the isles," Romeu said. "Once you get settled, I'll take you around and show you some of the best spots."

Ben grinned. After getting to know him, Ben had found another friend in the crocodile shifter. It was good timing too because his Eloise had spent the entire trip in bed with Nami.

George walked across the deck. "We're almost there, everyone. Shauna said folks would be there to bring your things home." He gave Ben a sympathetic look. "She said you and Dover have been ordered to appear before the royal court as soon as we arrive."

Kai frowned. "That can't be right. Surely Father will want to meet Ben before presenting him to the entire court. Talia said she explained the situation to him."

George shrugged. "I only know what Shauna told me."

Dover hugged Chubber and gave Ben a worried look. "If you would rather go on to the cottage, I'll make something up. I can say you're not feeling well and will attend court later."

Ben gave his mate a flat look. "Not happening. I go where you go, love."

Kai gave him a nod. "I'll be there too. I don't know what Father is thinking, but you two are mated now. There's not much he can do that is socially acceptable."

Ben arched a brow. "That's reassuring."

Eloise and Nami joined them on deck a few moments later. His friend looked decidedly rumpled and Ben couldn't help but grin. "How's the honeymoon phase working out?"

Eloise grinned back. "The bed is tiny, but you can't beat the company."

Nami rolled her eyes. "Mom texted. She's waiting at the docks for us, Dover."

Dover practically vibrated with excitement. "I can't wait for you to meet Shauna and Ervin, Ben. They'll love you."

Ben bent and kissed him, tongue sneaking a taste of his omega. "Me neither."

As the ship entered the bay, several merfolk swam alongside it, their guppy tails moving them quickly through the water as they kept pace with the ship.

"Prince Dover," one man called out, waving. "Did you really find your mate?"

"Hi, Moore," Dover said waving and grinning. "This is Ben. He's my human. Isn't he beautiful?"

Moore laughed, his purple tail flipping water as he dove down, then back up. "Hi, Ben. I tend the reefs around the bay. When you get settled, I'll dig up some snorkeling gear and take you on a tour."

Ben felt a knot of worry in his gut ease. "I'd like that. Thanks!" Dover's family may hate him, but at least there were mers on the isles that would be happy for Dover and him.

"Prince Dover," a mermaid waved. "The girls and I restocked your refrigerator and checked over your creek."

"Thank you, Siana," Dover said. "Have you seen my mate? Isn't he beautiful?"

Ben groaned and buried his face in his hands when Kai and Eloise laughed at him.

"Aww, leave him alone," Romeu said. "Benny boy can't help it that he's so darn cute."

Ben glared at the man.

"Romeu!" A mermaid with dark green hair and a guppy tail yelled from the water. "Nami told me you have a puppy. I thought we agreed no pets until Janie was out of diapers."

Ben grinned when his friend clutched Jojo to his chest before he stood up and looked over the rails. "Hey, hon. Jojo was gift from Prince Dover. I couldn't refuse to take her. That would be treason, right?"

His wife, Joy, glared at him. "That's nonsense. Now, give the puppy back to the prince."

Romeu gasped. "I can't return her. Jojo is family now. I already told her about the kids and we've bonded." He held her up. "Look at her, Joy. She's just a little baby."

Joy groaned. "Why did I mate you again?"

By the time they docked, Ben knew way too much about why Joy had mated Romeu. "There are some things you should keep to yourself," he told the shifter.

Romeu grinned and ran past him, eager to reach his wife. "I'll drive your truck to the cottage, Benny boy. I'll try not to put too many dents in it."

Dover chuckled and pulled Ben and Otis down the ramp. "Come on. Shauna should be right ---"

A pink-haired woman interrupted Dover with a shout. "Dover, Nami! Get over here and hug me right now." She pulled Dover and Nami to her, squishing them together as she hugged them. Chubber wiggled from between them and hopped to Otis' back, tittering in annoyance.

Ben exchanged a look with Eloise. They both were a little apprehensive about meeting Shauna.

Shauna released Dover and Nami and wiped her eyes. "I missed you two so much. I've gotten too used to having you both around." She turned to Ben and Eloise and looked them up and down. "These are your mates?"

"Isn't Ben beautiful?" Dover asked and wiggled back into his arms. "Look at his eyes, Shauna."

One side of Shauna's mouth turned up as she tried not to smile. "Your mate is lovely, bluetail."

She pulled Eloise and Ben into her arms, squishing them like she had Dover and Nami. "Eloise is lovely too. I'm sorry to hear your family didn't react well to you mating my Nami."

"It's cool," Eloise said, face squished against Ben's shoulder. "I have Ben and Uncle George."

"You have me too," Shauna said and kissed her cheek. She kissed Ben's next. "You both do."

"Your highness?" A small troop of guards approached and bowed their heads to Dover. "We've been ordered to escort you and the human to the castle."

Shauna gave Ben one more kiss. "Try to be respectful, but don't let them push you around," she whispered.

"I'll take care of your motorcycle," Eloise said, nodding.

"I'll take Velma to the cottage," Nami added, taking Otis' leash from Ben's hand. "Come on Otis and Chubs, you two are riding in the sidecar with Mom."

Kai patted his back. "Let's get this over with. Soon enough you and Dover will be alone."

"Thank the goddess," Dover said. "Do you know how hard it is to have sex when your room is right next to a stupid crocodile shifter's room?"

Kit came to stand beside them, a round cheeked little girl in his arms. "Pearl, ignore your Uncle Dover and meet Uncle Ben."

Pearl grinned at him, then buried her face in her daddy's neck. "Hi, Unki Benny," she mumbled.

Ben's heart melted. "Hey, sweetie. Your dress is pretty."

She peeked at him and smiled. "It yellow. I likes yellow."

The guard cleared his throat. "Prince Dover, I'm afraid we must go."

Dover groaned. "Alright. We're coming."

Ben squeezed Dover's hand and they made their way through the docks to a parked limo. A short, awkward ride later, they arrived at the picture perfect castle.

The gardens around the castle were well maintained, but next to the vibrancy of the docks, they seemed cold. Guards opened the front doors for them and an older merman dressed in a black shirt and sarong waited for them.

Dover whined and gripped Ben's hand before nodding at the man. "Ervin."

Ben barely muffled his curse. Dover wanted to hug his friend, but there were too many judgmental assholes watching. Mers lined the seating areas of the large entrance, eyes cold. Women dressed in filmy shirts and scanty sarongs mixed with young men in ornamental arm bands and longer sarongs. All wore way too much jewelry for a species that spent so much time in the water.

One large breasted blond smirked at them. "Come now, everyone. Welcome the guppy prince and his human." The aristocratic mers laughed, voices harsh.

Ben noticed Dover's wince at the title, but Ervin's reaction startled him. The castle steward looked proud. Romeu was right. The guppy tailed merfolk were proud of Dover.

Kai growled. "Lorelei, watch your mouth. Insulting your own family is beyond shameful."

The woman rolled her eyes. "His tail is shameful."

Ben pulled Dover's hand to his lips and kissed his palm. "It's no insult, Prince Kai. She clearly understands the honor of being one of the guppy tailed mers. I'm privileged to be mated to my guppy prince. His beauty and kindness has no rival." He met Lorelei's eyes. "Absolutely. No. Rival."

Lorelei snarled and stood up. "How dare you!"

Ervin stepped forward, practically purring. "Prince Dover, the royal court awaits you and your mate. Please follow me."

Ben's smile faded and he swallowed hard when he saw the heated look in Dover's eyes. His mate gave him a wicked smile. "You are so getting laid tonight."

Kai snorted and Kit covered Pearl's ears. "For the love of shellfish, Dover. Keep it in your pants."

The guards muffled their laughter and led them to a large room deep within the castle. They bowed and joined the other guards lining the side of the entrance.

Ervin's light touch slid across Ben's back. "Good luck, Prince Ben. We are honored to have you join the royal family."

Ben groaned at being called *prince* but Dover's smile lit up the room. "Thank you, Ervin."

Kai and Kit led them into the room and Ben

immediately felt the hostility aimed his way. The room was circular with several curved rows of seats. The first few rows were full of older merfolk, mostly men, but the last two rows held younger mers and was an equal mix of men and women.

No matter which row they sat on, each person looked at Ben like he was a bug on the bottom of their shoe.

King Ren looked like a mixture of Kit and Kai. He had the same broad, muscular build as Kai, but his hair, freckles, and facial features were almost identical to Kit. He sat on a cold, marble throne and an elaborate crown of gold, pearls, and white tulip seashells sat on his head.

Behind him stood a younger, red-haired woman who was clearly his daughter. She watched him sympathetically.

"Dover," King Ren said. "You were not authorized to leave Latch Bay."

"Father," Dover said, bowing. "I heard the mating call and went in search of my mate."

Ben followed his example and awkwardly bowed. "Hi, your majesty."

"You bring a human here," a merman said. He stood beside the King's throne and glared at Ben. "Humans are corrupt and destructive imbeciles. You disgrace your family name by mating with one."

From the corner of his eye, Ben noticed Dover massage his temple, as if he were getting a headache. He imagined if he had to deal with loudmouths like this too often, he'd get a headache too.

Ben narrowed his eyes on the stranger. "A person's species doesn't predetermine their trustworthiness. I imagine there are one or two mers that fit the description of a corrupt and destructive imbecile." He met the man's gaze, making no effort to hide what he thought of the asshole.

"The wretched human is clearly unworthy of the Rees name," the man said. "You Majesty, I advise you to order your son to marry one of the mermen on the list I gave you."

Kai scowled. "You would have Dover betray his mate, Lord Eades?"

Lord Eades smiled smugly. "If your king orders it, then it must be done." He smirked at Dover. "Alternatively, our beloved king could banish the guppy to live with other freaks in The Deep."

"Fuck you," Ben said, growling. "Dover is twice the man you are, you sorry piece of shit."

The room erupted in angry voices and Lord Eades' face turned purple. "Guards! Arrest the human."

"Enough, Lord Eades," the woman behind the king said, voice silencing the room. The guards turned to her, looking for clear orders. "You don't speak for our father and you are addressing a royal consort. Show some respect."

Ben kept his eyes on King Ren. The man's expression stayed completely emotionless, but Ben was sure there was something in his eyes. He couldn't say what it was, though. The king may be plotting to feed Ben to the Coalswell sharks for all he could read the man.

"You are dismissed," King Ren said, turning away from Dover. "We have more important items to discuss today. Several of you have suggested expanding the farms closer to The Deep. I will hear your reasoning now."

Kit grabbed Ben's arm and hustled them out the door. "Let's get while the getting's good."

Kai nodded at Ben, eyes troubled, then took a seat, clearly wanting to hear the discussion.

They left him behind and Dover released a deep breath once the doors shut behind them. "That could have gone better."

The guard closest to them winced. "Lord Eades' voice carries, your highness. I'd say this was a good day. Your mate could be in the dungeon right now."

CHAPTER 14

*D*over jumped from the stupid fancy limo and pulled Ben out behind him. He never went home by car, but he did actually have a driveway. It was overgrown and rough with disuse, but it still existed.

"We're home, Ben," he whispered, spinning to watch Ben's face as he looked over the cottage. The smell of the trees and flowers made Dover's head spin and he almost cried as he listened to the roar of the waterfall.

"Wait," Ben said, eyes narrowing on the front porch of the cottage.

Dover whimpered. Ben *had* to love the cottage. Dover desperately wanted his mate to be happy here. He was going to have to put up with stupid shit like today and there had to be something here to make it all worthwhile.

"Who packed the damn dick-shaped fountain? I thought we left that in South Carolina," Ben said, groaning.

The guard who had escorted them home started

laughing when Chubber and Shell looked up from where they were playing in the base of the fountain. Someone had already set it up in the corner of porch and water gurgled and flowed from the tip.

"It's part of Chubber's treasure," Dover said, shoulders sinking with relief. Maybe Ben didn't hate the cottage after all. Dover grabbed his hand and pulled Ben down the trail toward the creek. "You have to see the creek."

Otis barked and ran out of the open door, tail wagging. Dover stopped to pet him, then grabbed Ben's hand again. *Ben has to love my creek*, he thought. *He has to.*

Ben pulled him to a stop when they reached the waterfall and creek and his face filled with awe. "Dover, this is... I can see why you love it."

Dover pulled his shirt and sarong off and pulled Ben with him toward the water. "Let's swim."

Ben laughed and hurried to undress. "Okay, okay. I'm really glad it's warmer here than back at Aunt Prue's. I have the feeling we'll be in the water all the time."

Otis splashed into the creek, barking as he doggy paddled around in circles. Chubber darted up Ben's leg, then jumped from his shoulder and sailed through the air, gracefully diving into the water.

Shell chattered and climbed into Dover's arms. "Hey Shell. Chubber had fun, but he missed you while he was gone." He pressed his face into her back. "I missed you too."

Ben looked over his shoulder. "Hey, Shell. Chubber

is the best otter I've ever met. You did well with him, ma'am."

Shell leaned up and patted Ben's cheek, making Dover laugh. "Come on. Let's swim."

Dover ran into the water and called his tail. *My creek! My home.* The fresh, crisp taste of the water was so good. He dove deep and spun around in circles, enjoying the cool depths. A turtle and a few fish swam past him and he sighed, bubbles rising to the surface. *Home.*

He saw Ben dive down and swim toward him, arms and legs moving smoothly through the water. His human was so sexy, but Dover wished Ben had ditched the underwear.

Splashing drew his attention and he saw Otis and Chubber swimming at the surface. Then he noticed Jojo and the large crocodile she swam with. Maybe it was good thing Ben left his underwear on.

Ben reached him, face looking funny as he held his breath. He stroked a hand through Dover's hair, then trailed his fingers down Dover's tail.

"You really love me, don't you?" Dover asked, knowing Ben couldn't understand or answer him. With the way his mate looked at him, he didn't have to answer Dover.

Ben stroked his face, then leaned forward and kissed Dover. Dover breathed into Ben's mouth, sharing the air his merform created. They had created a routine on their swims. Ben would swim as deep as was safe and Dover would make sure he didn't drown.

A beaver swam past him and he startled. He had only seen Eloise shifted when they met Prince Tack.

Nami swam after her mate, laughing. "Look at her, bluetail. Isn't she amazing?"

Dover blinked. She was a beaver. He didn't know what was amazing about that. It's not like Eloise had broad shoulders, and sweet brown eyes. Her smile didn't turn his innards to fire. "Yeah. She's okay."

He leaned over and kissed Ben again, letting his tongue explore his mate's mouth.

"Unki Benny." Pearl swam between them and booped Dover in the gut with her butt. "Play with me."

Ben gave Dover a heated look, then swam after the little girl.

"Remember to keep him near the surface, Pearl," Kit said, swimming by them. "Hey, Dover. Hope you don't mind sharing your creek."

Dover glared at him. "Remember when everyone ignored me? Can we go back to that for a couple of weeks?"

Kit hugged him. "Nope. Your house is full of guppy tails, you know. You have a lot of friends that want to congratulate you."

Dover blinked a couple of times. "Really?"

"Ervin and his husband are helping Shauna cook a huge meal." Kit spun him around, his clownfish tail swishing in the water. "I envy you, Dover."

"You envy *me*?" Dover shook his head. "What is wrong with you?"

"You don't even notice how many friends you have," Kit said, laughing. "How did you possibly think you could be gone a whole month before we'd notice?"

"You don't visit often," Dover said, pouting.

"I visit you every other week," Kit said. "When I don't come to you, we meet each other at the reefs for a swim. I know, because I try not to bother you too much. You like your quiet."

"I thought..." Dover trailed off. He had thought Kit merely tolerated him.

"I know what you thought," Kit said, huffing, when Ben pushed between them.

Dover laughed, then kissed his mate, sharing his breath. Ben stroked his cheek, then took off after Pearl again.

He dodged out of Romeu's way when the crocodile headed for the bottom of the creek to sulk. Two little mers and a tiny crocodile shifter had taken Jojo away from him. Romeu's kids apparently approved of the new puppy. They would give Jojo all the love her witch should have given her.

His creek was filling with mers and Dover couldn't stop his smile. He met Kit's stare. "Okay. I'm a mopey idiot. I'm sorry that I didn't let you know how much you mean to me. I love you, Pearl, and Kai so much."

Kit grinned. "Good. Nami is swimming this way with her beaver. Let's ambush them."

Dover hummed, pleased. "Perfect."

An hour later, Shauna made them all leave the creek and return to the house.

Dover smiled softly when he saw a delicate gold bracelet decorated with tiny white tulip shells and creamy white pearls lying on his dark blue sarong. The small, gold clasp was a tiny guppy fish. *Looks like Kai or Kit are back to leaving gifts.*

"Where did that come from?" Ben asked, nodding appreciatively. "It's a nice piece."

Dover fastened it on his wrist and shrugged. "Someone leaves me jewelry pretty often. I think Kai or Kit plunder the royal treasury every once in a while and bring me all the guppy themed jewelry."

Ben looked thoughtful. "That's nice of them."

Dover sniffed the air and ran up the path. "I smell shrimp."

With Ervin's help, Shauna had cooked a feast of grilled fish and shrimp and steamed crab legs. It was spread across several picnic tables that Dover didn't remember having.

Eloise and Nami helped unload chairs from an unfamiliar truck and Dover pushed his mate into one. Ben looked worn out. The emotional ups and downs of the day were catching up to both of them, and Dover knew Ben wasn't used to playing so hard. Pearl was a little demon in the water.

Ervin's mate, Owin, set a platter of corn cobs on one of the tables next to a few platters of different types of greens and diced fruit. He gave Dover a big hug, then eyed Ben. "Hey. I'm Ervin's mate, Owin. I brought you a chicken."

Dover hid his smile when Ben looked confused. Owin was a strange one. "A chicken?"

Owin nodded, smiling wide. "Yeah. This morning, I

looked up humans from the southern U.S. and the internet says one of your favored foods is fried chicken. We mostly eat seafood here, so I brought you a chicken."

"A whole chicken?" Ben blinked, looking dazed.

"Yes, it's walking around here somewhere," Owin said, frowning as he looked around. "Oh, there it is." He pointed across the yard where Otis was sniffing a small, plump chicken with creamy white and red feathers. "It'll make a good meal. Let me know if you want more. There's a mer that raises them. He lives close to The Deep."

"Thank you?" Ben watched Otis lick the chicken's head while it stared around the yard. Dover had a feeling they wouldn't be having chicken for dinner. While Ben was alright with fishing, he didn't like the idea of hunting his food. He preferred buying it in a grocery store.

Dover shrugged. Humans were strange. Ervin came out and Dover ran to the man. He wanted his hugs and he wanted them now.

"Hey, did you make that waterfall glass picture thing?" Owin asked Ben.

Ben nodded, then grinned. "Did you recognize the pearl?"

Owin grinned. "Yeah. My Ervin loves his pearls. I can't believe Prince Dover kept his so long."

Dover looked up from where he was hugging Ervin as if his life depended on it. "Ervin taught me how to treasure."

The royal steward flushed. "You were well on your

way to mastering that already, bluetail." He kissed Dover's cheek, then went back inside.

Owin watched him go, then bit his lip. "I was wondering how much it would cost to have you make something for Ervin. Our anniversary is coming up and I want to get him something special."

Ben smiled softly. "For Ervin, I'll make you a deal. If you find the items you want in the picture, I'll put it together. I have an idea of what I want to make the man that was so kind to my mate. I just need some personal treasures to put in there."

Owin frowned. "I can pay."

Ben shrugged. "You don't pay me, Owin. Your mate means a lot to my guppy prince."

Dover covered his mouth, eyes watering. The title that had hurt him for so long sounded like the highest of compliments coming from his mate. He thought back to Lorelai's angry expression when Ben stood up to her today.

Owin smiled shyly. "I'll start collecting shells tomorrow. I have a few pearls I've found over the years that I'd like to include too."

Ervin came back out with two platters of rice. "Owin, go get more corn."

Owin saluted, then leaned in and kissed his mate. "Yes, sir."

Ervin blushed, then laughed and pushed his mate toward the door. "Get moving."

Dover slid into Ben's lap. "Do you like our home?"

Ben bit Dover's neck, gentle and teasing. "I haven't actually seen inside the house, but I love your creek."

"Our creek," I corrected, breathing his scent in.

"Our home will make me happy as long as you're in it," Ben said quietly. "Your sister is coming this way."

Dover looked up, fast. Talia stopped in front of them. She nodded at Ben. "Welcome to the Southern Silver Isles. I'm sorry you had to appear in court as soon as you docked. Lord Eades was insistent."

Ben gave her a wry look. "I got the impression Lord Eades is an asshole."

She grinned. "You'd be right." She looked at Dover. "Dover, can I speak with you alone?"

Dover made a face. "I'm comfortable."

Talia arched a brow.

"Alright," he said, groaning as he stood. He bent and kissed Ben. "Otis is napping with your chicken."

Ben looked to where Otis was curled around the chicken, snoring. "Damn it. I'm going to have to build a chicken house, aren't I?"

A few of the guppy tailed mers came to sit with Ben. "Don't worry, Ben. We'll help you build a nice house for your chicken," Moore said, frowning. "I don't understand why you want to build it a house when you could just eat it, though."

Dover laughed at the look on Ben's face, then followed Talia. Once they were a distance from the large group of people, he turned to face her. "What's going on?"

Her expression was serious. "Is he really your mate?" she asked bluntly.

Dover nodded. "I heard the mating call and it led me to him."

Her eyes seemed to search his face. "Do you truly love him, Dover?"

"More than anything in the world," he said.

She nodded, eyes hardening. "You need to start coming to court, but Ben should avoid it as much as possible. We need you to give the guppy tails a voice, but we don't want to make your mate more of a target than he already is."

"Talia, what's going on?"

A look of pain flashed across her face. "Father has been more distant than usual."

"That's not saying a lot," Dover said, snorting.

"No," Talia said, shaking her head. "Father and I spoke all the time. As soon as I could walk, he's been training me to inherit the throne. He wants me to be a good ruler for our people. Now, though, Lord Eades is always with him. It's like he wants to keep me away from Father."

"The curse?" Dover twisted his fingers in his sarong. "Will Father try to hurt you?"

Talia closed her eyes. "I don't know. Even a year ago, I would have said that he would never hurt any of us. Now, I think he sees me as a threat to his power."

"Can you talk to him?"

"I can't get him alone," Talia said. "Lord Eades and his cronies are *always* there."

"What about Mother?" Dover tried not to think about the fact that his mother hadn't been there to greet him and Ben.

"Mother is too busy with Eugenia's wedding to care about anything else," Talia said. "Just... tell Ben to avoid court. Lord Eades is trying to make your mating look like a rebellion. He's telling everyone that your mate is a wicked human here to destroy the Silver Isles."

"Seriously? What idiot would believe him?"

"An idiot that hates humans because they tried to destroy the seas," Talia said, sighing. "Father isn't the only one that is paranoid of humans."

"Thank you, Talia." He leaned forward and hugged her. He had never hugged Talia before. She had always seemed as distant as their father. "We'll be careful."

She froze in place, then awkwardly returned his hug. "Congratulations, Dover. I'm truly happy for you. I'll do everything I can to protect you and your mate."

LATER THAT NIGHT, Dover's friends finally left.

Moore and his buddies had put together a wooden chicken house for Rachael, Ben's chicken. It looked more like a dog house, but Ben had decorated it with little strings of bright glass and beads. Now, Rachael roosted on a short bar within the small house.

Shauna and Ervin had made sure all the leftovers were put away and they had all worked together to clean up help Dover and Ben unpack. Now, Ben's beautiful art was mixed in with the knickknacks and shinies that Dover had been forced to leave behind.

Then, there was finally blessed peace. Shauna shooed everyone out the door. Otis settled in to sleep on the couch with Chubber, and Dover finally had Ben to himself.

"My mate," Dover said, climbing the stairs. "Come look at our home."

Ben looked around the downstairs. "This really is home, isn't it? It's you and me."

Dover nodded. "I need to show you our bedroom. It's the best room in the house."

Ben gave him an amused look. "Really?" He followed Dover up the stairs.

"We have four bedrooms here," Dover said, opening the first door on the right. "This is our room."

Ben didn't take time to admire the décor. Dover laughed when his mate picked him up and laid him on the bed.

"It's been days since I've been in you," Ben said, voice hoarse. He pulled at the knot of Dover's sarong. "I like that you just wear a sarong everywhere. They're easy to remove." His hand slid up Dover's hip. "Or get around." Ben kissed Dover and his body sank against Dover's smaller one.

Dover ran his hands across Ben's back. His human felt so good. Their movements sped up as their dicks hardened and pressed against each other.

Ben took his time stretching Dover's hole, then pushed inside in one, strong thrust. They moved together, setting a fast rhythm that Dover couldn't resist.

Ben hit just the right spot and Dover cried out, coming all over his stomach. He felt the heat of Ben's cum fill his ass when his mate found his own release.

"Damn, bluetail," Ben said, sounding winded. "The things you do to me."

Dover smiled against Ben's shoulder. "Our bedroom also has a master bathroom."

Ben laughed. "Is that your way of telling me to go get a washcloth?"

"I like it when you clean me up," Dover said, admitting to himself that maybe he *was* a little too lazy.

Ben went to the bathroom and got a wet cloth. He smiled and wiped Dover off, pausing at the small curve of his stomach.

"I'm not getting fat, Ben," Dover said, smiling. "You know omegas almost always conceive during their heat."

A grin spread across Ben's face. "We're having a baby?"

"I think so," Dover said, smiling brightly. "I wanted to see a doctor before I said anything, but I haven't had time. Romeu said I smelled different. You know how good shifter noses are."

Ben picked Dover off the bed and spun him around the room. "We're having a baby! Fuck, now our wedding needs to happen fast. I want to be your husband before the baby gets here."

Dover put his arms around Ben's neck and chuckled as his mate danced him around the room. He'd go see the doctor tomorrow. Before he attended court. Talia and Kai were right. He needed to be his friends' voice. He was their guppy prince.

CHAPTER 15

*B*en scratched his belly and looked around the house. He didn't fully understand how this place already felt like home. Ben thought maybe this was what he had been searching for his whole life.

It was barely past dawn, but Dover had already left, determined to speak with Ervin before attending court. Chubber had put Dover's crown around his waist and insisted on going with.

Ben had also wanted to go, even if just to see the king's court react to the otter wearing a crown, but Dover had begged him to stay here. *Damn those sweet blue eyes*, he thought. He would do anything Dover asked him to do.

Otis watched him from the couch. The dog was convinced it was too early to get up, even for breakfast.

"I guess I'm a house-husband now, Otis." Ben sighed. "I'll work on my glass art and raise our chicken."

A loud squawk drew Ben's attention to the

window. He peeked outside and saw a merman in his early forties in their front yard. He wore the plain black sarong of the castle servants, but Ben didn't recognize him from yesterday. The man had dark hair and average features that would blend perfectly in a crowd.

The stranger danced away from Rachael. Ben's chicken waved her wings and squawked again.

"Good guard chicken," Ben whispered, then glared at Otis.

His dog laid his head down and closed his eyes, falling back to sleep.

The man hopped onto the rail of the porch. "Get back, demon."

Rachael flapped her wings and flew up to the rail, and the man screeched, falling from the porch.

Ben opened the door. "Rachael, that's enough."

His chicken clucked at him, then settled down on the rail and closed her eyes.

Ben helped the omega stand up. "Hi. I'm sorry, but I don't recognize you."

The man's eyes darted around and he bit his lip nervously. "Oh. I'm Fergus. I work at the castle."

"Can I help you, Fergus?" Ben asked, then noticed the slender crown in Fergus' hand. It was made of silver and covered with coffee bean seashells interspersed with chocolate pearls.

Fergus groaned and danced from foot to foot. "You weren't supposed to see me."

Ben narrowed his eyes. "Are you the one leaving the jewelry for Dover?"

Fergus didn't have to answer. Ben saw the guilt in his eyes.

"Explain yourself, Fergus," Ben said, voice as stern as he could make it.

Fergus groaned and closed his eyes. "I can't tell you who I serve. I bring items to Dover as requested. That's all." He handed Ben the crown. "This one is actually for you. It's a consort's crown."

Ben took it, thoughts churning. "You don't work for Kai or Kit, do you?" They wouldn't have hesitated to give him the crown themselves.

"No." Fergus lifted his chin. "That is all I will say. Have a good day, your highness, and please consider eating the demon chicken soon." He spun around and headed down the trail toward the waterfall.

Ben picked up Rachael and tucked her under his arm before following Fergus. "Do you work for Talia?"

Fergus glared over his shoulder. "I won't say, your highness."

"What about Ervin?"

Fergus rolled his eyes and stomped to the stairway carved into the rock wall next to the waterfall. "Your shifter friends are coming now, your highness."

Ben looked the other way, eyes following the creek as it ran toward the lake. Sure enough, a crocodile swam slowly down the middle of the creek. A beaver with a pack sat on the crocodile's back and munched a stick.

"Don't distract me, Fergus," Ben said, turning back to the stairs. "Damn it."

The man was long gone.

Ben turned and walked back to the cottage. He put Rachael on top of her house and put the crown on his head.

"I feel stupid," he told the chicken.

"You look kinda stupid," Eloise said, laughing and she pulled a t-shirt on. "Fuck munches, Benny, you're wearing a crown and talking to a chicken."

"I think you look distinguished," Romeu said, straightening his own quickly donned shorts.

"Thank you," Ben said, sniffing.

"Oh." Romeu gave him a sympathetic look. "I was talking to your chicken."

Ben scowled and pulled the crown off. "A servant named Fergus dropped it off. He works for someone in the castle."

Romeu shrugged. "Never heard of him. Get your ass in gear, Benny boy. We're going on a tour of the Southern Isles today."

Ben arched a brow and led them in the house. "The whole Southern Isles?"

Romeu grinned, teeth looking extra sharp. "I never told you what I do, did I?"

"Nope."

"I fly shipments of pearls from the farms all over the isles to the warehouses in Latch Bay. I have a nice little plane waiting to fly your asses around today."

Eloise grabbed Otis' leash. "Come on, boy. You're coming too. We gotta see our new home, buddy."

"She's a lot nicer to Otis," Ben said, slipping on a pair of flip flops and setting the crown on the kitchen counter.

"He's cuter," Romeu said with a shrug. "You'll have to drive us to the runway."

They piled in Ben's truck and Ben drove down the rough, overgrown driveway. "What are we seeing today?"

"Just the highlights," Romeu said. There are six cities in the kingdom and several good-sized towns. Believe it or not, quite a few merfolk live under the islands. There are thousands of caves along the coasts and they've gotten good about modernizing. My buddy, Sako, has a four bedroom cave with plumbing, electricity, and internet. Crazy, right?"

"How do people get there?" Ben asked, shaking his head.

"They swim or they don't go," Romeu said, shrugging. "You are the only human living here, Benny boy."

Ben pondered that thought until they reached the small runway. Romeu's plane was a small cargo plane, but it had plenty of space for all of them.

They were in the air in no time, and Ben couldn't help but feel awe at the beauty of the land below him. The islands had clean, white sand beaches; thick, green forests; and beautiful, clean lakes. The city of Latch Bay spread out along the shores of the bay with low, glass and stone buildings and straight, well maintained roads.

Romeu flew further inland and Ben watched as mist covered mountains filled his view.

"Not a lot of merfolk live in the mountains," Romeu said. "The ones that do prefer the fresh water of the streams and rivers that flow down into the lakes. There are a shit load of sprites in there, though."

Otis settled between Ben's legs and barked at the window as they flew high over a mountain peak.

Ben pressed his face to the window, eyes widening. A wispy air sprite flew alongside the plane, blending with the mist shrouding the mountains. The creature's eyes were full of white and grey smoke and it smiled at him and waved.

"Fuck me," he whispered, waving back.

"No, thanks," Eloise said, leaning in to watch the sprite. "This place is gorgeous. I have no job anymore, but I don't give a beaver's dam. I could just explore all day long."

"We'll find you work," Romeu said. "Nami works in the pearl farms and her mom still works part-time at the castle, but you probably wouldn't enjoy any of those jobs. We have a few construction companies here, and I've asked around. I'll let you know what I hear."

"You're the best, Romeu." Eloise bumped Ben's head with her own. "He's my best friend now."

"I'm sorry, I don't have connections," Ben said. "I'm just an artist raising his chicken."

After a few hours, they reached the end of the Southern Silver Isles.

Romeu circled the plane around. "Out there is The Deep. It's miles and miles of ocean that no ship crosses. The hippocampi herds love it, but no mer goes out there and comes back."

"That's where the tentacle tailed merfolk live?" Eloise asked.

"Huh?" Ben hadn't heard anything about tentacles.

Romeu started to lower the plane. "There's a nice stripe of land right here. There's something I have to check."

Ben exchanged a look with Eloise. "Romeu, what's going on?"

The crocodile was quiet as he landed the plane, then he turned to them. "Okay, so you remember Prince Kai talking about the Sea Witch's curse?"

"Yeah," Ben said.

"All the merfolk from The Kingdom of the Deep are tentacle tailed. Some have jellyfish tentacles, some have squid tentacles, some have octopus tentacles. The thing is, they *all* have tentacles. At least, all the ones that have been seen."

"Okay?" Eloise said slowly. "What's the problem?"

"Before the curse, the merfolk of The Deep intermarried with merfolk from the Southern Isles. That means some families still occasionally pop out a tentacle tailed baby," Romeu said.

Personally, Ben thought a tentacle tailed baby sounded adorable. He wondered what his baby would look like. He hoped it was a guppy tailed mer like Dover.

"I'm still not seeing the problem," Eloise said, tilting her head and staring at Romeu.

"Right after the curse, the Southern Isles were a mess," Romeu said. "Joy told me families were torn apart because of the curse. The King was furious that

THE GUPPY PRINCE

his sister's kingdom was out of his reach and he knew her curse couldn't be avoided. He exiled all the tentacle tailed merfolk in his kingdom to The Deep. For several generations, any born as a tentacle tail was sent away."

"Fuck," Eloise said, shaking her head. "That's terrible."

"That don't do that anymore," Ben said. "Right?"

Romeu was quiet. "You two will figure out soon enough, but mer babies are born human. No matter if they're conceived in merform or human form, they're always born human."

Ben held his hand up. "Back up a second. Merfolk can have sex in their merforms?"

Romeu blushed. "Yeah. Fuck, when I first came here on spring break, there was a heat swarm. All the single omegas in heat gathered in the sea right outside of Latch Bay and alphas showed up and made it a big merfolk orgy. If I hadn't already met Joy, I would have been on the first boat back home."

Ben's mouth dropped open. "A heat swarm? How did I not know about this?"

"Nami isn't going to any orgy," Eloise said, growling. "Not happening."

"You two wouldn't know, because you can't fuck your mates in merform because you *don't have* a merform. Plus, it's not like they have to attend the heat swarm," Romeu said, face completely red at this point. "It happens once a year and some mers go while some don't. That's how Kit got pregnant with Pearl. His parents were so pissed."

Ben groaned and covered his face. "Fuck, now I'm

seeing it. This is what happens when I start to see them as humans with a fish tail. I forget I'm a completely different species."

Romeu cleared his throat. "Back to what I was saying, my eldest girls were born human. Around four to six months, a mer baby has its first shift. It's called their tailday and that's what they celebrate instead of a birthday."

Ben made a mental note to ask Dover when his tailday was. It was things like this that reminded him that he had only known Dover for about two months.

"Okay," Eloise said. "I'm still stuck on heat swarms. What if they're shark tailed? Do they have two penises? I didn't study the Coalswells that closely." She pulled her phone out. "I'm texting Kai."

Romeu started laughing. "He really shouldn't have given you his number for emergencies."

Ben sighed and tried to act like he didn't care about Kai's answer. "So, what happens if a baby ends up with a tentacle tail?"

Romeu nodded. "That was my whole point in stopping here. Things have gotten a lot better. Tentacle tailed merfolk aren't exiled. I had a buddy who's youngest is tentacle tailed. They weren't forced to do anything, but he lost his job in the castle and the lord that was in charge of his village started making things uncomfortable. He ended up moving to the mountains."

"That sucks," Eloise said. "I bet when Princess Talia inherits, that shit won't happen anymore."

"I think so," Romeu said. "My friend's experience

was a good one compared to most. Some families don't want to deal with the trouble of having a tentacle tailed baby."

Ben looked out the window of the plane. The tiny island they had landed on was mostly bare. There was a stand of trees to their right, but that was it. "Romeu, why are we here?"

"When a family doesn't want the baby, they bring it here," Romeu said. "There's a shallow pool of water right at the edge of the beach. Someone from The Deep checks the pool every day. Prince Kai sends patrols here often to check the pool. If they find a little one, the guards wait until someone comes from The Deep."

Eloise looked like she was about to explode. "What. The. Fuck."

Ben unbuckled his seatbelt and jumped up. "Let me out. We need to check that pool. Are there any predators on the island?"

Romeu unbuckled his seatbelt. "I always check when I'm out this way. It doesn't happen often, but Joy's brother was here once when it did. No one wants a baby to have to wait by itself."

They left the plane and Romeu started to lead them toward the trees. Romeu and Eloise both gasped at the same time, looking at one another in horror.

"Do you hear that?" Eloise asked.

Ben pushed past them and started running. As he got closer, he heard a baby crying and ran faster.

The pool was small and shaded by the trees. In the middle of the pool was a baby who looked to be about five or six months old. His small, brown tentacles contracted and relaxed, keeping him upright and his head above the water. The baby's bottom lip trembled and he held his arms out to Ben as he cried.

"I'm coming, baby boy," Ben said, wading into the pool and sinking down until he sat on the sandy bottom, his head and shoulders above the water.

The baby swam to him and Ben wrapped him in his arms. "Shh, baby boy. I'm here."

His little body shook with his wails and Ben's heart broke. He rubbed circles on the boy's back, singing softly under his breath and the boy settled his head against Ben's shoulder.

He's my baby now, Ben thought. *Dover and I know treasure when we see it.*

Splashing drew his attention and he looked over his shoulder. Otis splashed toward him, Romeu and Eloise right behind him.

"Holy shit," Romeu said, looking furious. "I can't believe someone really did this. It's one thing to know it can happen, but fuck."

The baby's cries quieted and his breathes evened out. Ben felt tentacles wrap around his waist as the boy clung to him.

"Does he have a bag anywhere?" Ben looked around. "I don't have any baby stuff at the house."

Otis doggy paddled beside him and reached out to lick the baby, making the boy giggle against Ben's shoulder.

Romeu sank beside him. "You're taking him home instead of waiting here for someone from The Deep?"

Eloise sat on his other side and smiled at the baby.

"Fuck yeah, he is. If he won't, then I will. I think Nami's pregnant, but so is Dover. Either way this little buddy is getting parents and a little unborn sibling."

"You know Dover's pregnant?" Ben asked. "You smelled it, didn't you? Why didn't you say anything?"

Eloise gave him a sheepish look. "Meeting Nami kind of distracted me."

Ben gave her a look, then stood, lifting the baby with him. The little boy's tentacles shifted into legs and Ben adjusted his grip and looked out at the ocean.

About twenty feet offshore a woman with stark white hair and pale skin watched him above the water. She looked to be in her mid-forties and wore a strange crown of twisting dark purple coral and black pearls. Long strands of black pearls hung around her neck and down the front of her body. He knew without asking that she was a mermaid from The Deep.

He waded out of the pool and walked toward the surf. "Hi, ma'am. I'll take care of this one. Alright? My mate and I will give him all the love he needs."

She smiled and her eyes danced with delight. "Finally."

Ben tilted his head. "Huh?"

The woman turned and dove into the waves. Thick black tentacles arched out of the water before disappearing.

"That was a lot of expensive jewelry for some random mermaid," Eloise said quietly. "Her smell was... powerful, Benny. I'm kinda turned on and kinda creeped out."

Ben ignored her. "Romeu, give me your shirt. This baby needs a diaper."

"Why my shirt?" Romeu pouted, but pulled his t-shirt off.

"Because I'm a prince consort," Ben said, nose in the air.

"Don't let him fool you, Romeu. That's just one of his favorite shirts," Eloise said, laughing. "Let's get this baby home. I'll text Shauna and ask her if she knows where to get baby stuff."

Romeu scoffed. "Forget that. I've got boxes of shit from when Janie was this little bit's age. I'll fly you all home, then go get it."

Dover cuddled the boy closer, hating the little whimpers he made as he clung to Dover. Someone needed their ass kicked.

Eloise's phone dinged and she looked at it. "Kai has two penises. Just so you know."

CHAPTER 16

*D*over wanted to beat his head against the stone wall of his Father's throne room. Chubber was already passed out asleep in Dover's lap.

"Budgetary policy nine point six establishes a precedence to redistribute the funds between Lord Justinian and Lady Belinda." The lord with the driest, most monotone voice in the world looked around the room. "I call for a motion to dismiss the civil suit and allow the two to continue with their plan to establish management of the new pearl farm."

Dover turned his head slowly and glared at Kai. "I thought you said this meeting would cover important things," he whispered.

"It will," Kai said from the side of his mouth. "Give it time."

"I hate you so much."

"Ah, I love you, little brother."

Dover turned back to the meeting and watched his father. As usual, the King's face was as expressionless as a statue. Sometimes Dover thought his father really was a statue. Then, he would give an order and Dover wished the man *was* just a statue.

Talia sat to King Ren's right and seemed engrossed in the discussion. Dover was glad she was the heir. He couldn't deal with this shit every day.

Three more of their siblings sat in different spots around the room and Dover was happy to see they were as bored as he was. Kit and the rest of his brothers and sisters were absent and Dover wished he was with them.

"The civil suit claims that the funds were already given to Trix and Holli Mulhona," Talia said. "Why exactly do you think those funds should go to Lord Justinian and Lady Belinda? All policy nine point six states is that allocated funds only go to approved sources."

The merman sputtered. "Your highness, the Mulhonas aren't capable of running a pearl farm at that scale."

Dover frowned. He knew Trix and Holli. "Yes, they are. Trix and Holli have both contributed to the management of pearl farms their whole lives. I'd say that they're actually far more suitable than Lord Justinian and Lady Belinda."

"Overseeing the workers isn't the same thing as managing, Prince Dover," Lady Belinda said, smiling at the other nobles. "This is why Lord Justinian and I have stepped in."

Dover glared at her. "Trix kept the northwest pearl farm running while you, Lady Belinda, sat on your ass here at the castle for *years*, reaping in the profits of his hard work. Holli has brought in more trade agreements through her work with oversea clients than anyone in the past ten years. What exactly do you bring beside a title and an ego to match?"

Lady Belinda stuttered, flushing with embarrassment.

Lord Eades stood up. "Of course, the guppy prince would want us to give millions to two guppy tailed workers. Just keep quiet, Prince Dover. There's a reason your father wanted you married and breeding instead of sitting in on important discussions."

The King didn't even hitch a breath at Eades' ugly words. A familiar heavy buzzing filled Dover's head. He had felt it before. Every time he attended court and his father let Lord Eades or one of the others insult him or the other guppy tailed mers it felt like cotton was stuffed in his ears. It seemed louder now.

Dover hated feeling small and insignificant. He petted Chubber's back, fighting the urge to leave the room. *That won't do Trix and Holli any good*, he told himself.

"Lord Eades, I know exactly what I'm talking about," Dover said. "I also make a motion to proceed with the civil suit. Lady Belinda and Lord Justinian are trying to profit off the hard work of others and can't be trusted with that much money. The Mulhona siblings were determined to be a good investment when King Ren signed the grant. There is absolutely no reason to try to take those funds from them out of greed and prejudice."

"I second the motion," Kai said jovially. "I don't personally know the Mulhonas, but I trust my brother's judgment and the grant committee's original decision."

Talia smiled serenely. "Shall we vote?"

It was a very close call, but Dover was surprised the majority voted to proceed with the civil suit that the Mulhona siblings had filed against the two nobles when they tried to swoop in and take control of the funds.

Lord Eades stood again, practically glowering. "I think this is a good time to bring up the next issue on the agenda. Prince Dover has brought a human to *live* in our kingdom. This is unacceptable. Humans cannot be trusted. We all know their cruelty and their blatant disregard of living creatures. It is because of humans that the hippocampi were almost extinct. Us merfolk have brought their numbers back. We cannot have a human living amongst us."

Dover gave the man a flat look. "Not every human is bad, just like not every mer is good. You sound like a bigoted idiot."

You are a bigoted idiot, Dover thought to himself.

"How dare you," Lord Eades said, drawing himself up. "You show no respect to those far wiser than you. This just proves your judgment can't be trusted."

The buzzing grew louder and Dover rubbed his head, hoping he didn't get another headache.

"Lord Eades," Talia said, glaring at the man. "Ben Elliot is Prince Dover's true mate. If any stranger can possibly be trusted, it would be a mate."

"I've done a full background check on him," Kai said, shooting Dover an apologetic look. "There is no history of violence or cruelty. He will make a good addition to our bloodlines."

"Bloodlines," Lady Belinda said, looking suitably horrified. "Please tell me you don't plan to breed with him, Prince Dover."

Dover's eye twitched, but he didn't dive across the room and strangle the bitch. "I'm already pregnant, Belinda, and I'm quite proud to carry my mate's young."

Lord Eades gave him a smug look. "I'm not convinced, Prince Dover should breed at all. Perhaps we should discuss this in more detail."

Dots clouded his vision as the buzzing grew to a roar. Dover looked at his father. Nothing.

"This topic is not up for discussion," Talia said, snarling. "Dover and Ben are mated and are expecting. Move on, Lord Eades."

"We need to discuss revising our trade agreements with Belize," King Ren finally spoke. "Lord Eades, what are your thoughts?"

Dover sank back in his chair, the buzzing instantly gone. He couldn't believe they would even suggest that Ben was some kind of monster. He was a loving and sweet mate and would make a damn fine father.

Chubber looked at him and patted his knee. He was right. There was no need to make a scene right now. He'd have to talk to Kai and Talia about the problem later.

Hours later, Dover finally escaped the room. Kai

had left to deal with something with the guard and Talia had followed their father and Lord Eades to a conference room.

Dover quickly left the upper castle and shifted to swim through the lower castle. He needed to speak with his mother.

He found her with her ladies in one of the swimming rooms. Eugenia swam beside her, looking sullen.

Queen Kelby gave him a tight smile. "Dover."

"Mother," he said, nodding. "Can I speak with you for a moment?"

"Very well." She nodded to her ladies and followed him to a corner. "What do you want?"

He swallowed, hating feeling like he owed her anything. "Are you terribly angry with me?"

"I told you to forget the mating call," she hissed. "Yet you went anyway and brought back a human. A human, Dover. Do you know what my parents told me when I said my mate was a guppy tail?"

Dover bit his lip. "What?"

"They told me that nobles of the Southern Silver Isles have a responsibility to their titles. They must breed strong and honorable children of good bloodlines," she said, voice hard.

Dover covered his bare abdomen. "Your tail doesn't make you strong and honorable, Mother. I'm a guppy tail."

"Yes," she said, snarling, "and you're weak and traitorous. You ran from your home and returned with one of our enemies. I should have abandoned you to The Deep on your first tailday."

Dover's tears mixed with the water around them. "Mother, how can you say that?"

She looked uncertain for a moment, then her face hardened. "It's the truth. You are in for a rude surprise if you think your human is a good choice of a mate. Do us all a favor and stay away from the castle. Live in your shack and leave us in peace."

Dover turned and swam away, ignoring Eugenia as she called out to him. He clutched Chubber to him and swam as fast as he could.

"Dover, damn it, stop." A hand grabbed his arm and nails dug into his skin.

He turned to face Eugenia. "What do you want?"

"I heard what she said," Eugenia said, voice soft. "She's wrong, Dover. I don't want to marry Weston and I really don't want to have his children. He's a shitty person even if he is a noble. You heard the mating call and that is sacrosanct."

Dover sniffed. "I love Ben. He's a really good person."

She smiled sadly. "Good. You know that you're not the only one that Mother and Father ignore, right? Father doesn't speak to any of us except Talia and Mother takes nagging to a whole new level. All they care about is keeping up appearances so the nobles don't start complaining that the royal family is unfit."

Dover couldn't believe he was having this conversation with Eugenia. "I'm sorry, Eugenia. I got so wrapped up in my own misery I didn't even notice anyone else's and I should have. I *saw* how they treated Kit when he participated in the heat swarm."

Eugenia wrinkled her nose. "Don't remind me. Most of us envy you, Dover. You get to live away from all the old, judgmental nobles. Lord Eades and Lady Belinda in particular watch every move we make."

Dover squeezed her hand. "I thought you wanted to marry Weston. If you don't, then you shouldn't."

"Mother is insistent," Eugenia said. "She's already looking for Lorelai's husband now and goddess help whoever she chooses. I think Mother wants to marry us all off before the Coalswell prince can marry one of us."

"You're only twenty-four," Dover said. "You have plenty of time to get married."

Eugenia shrugged then changed the subject. "Are you going to have a wedding or did you already have one back in the U.S.?"

"Ben wants a wedding," Dover said, smiling. "It surprises me, but it's what he wants."

"Then we'll have one," Eugenia said, grinning. "It probably shouldn't be at the castle. Lord Eades would have a stroke. I'll talk with our event coordinator about a good location."

"I want to get married at my creek," Dover said. "It's the best place on the island."

Eugenia rolled her eyes. "Of course, you would say that. Alright. Leave the clothing to me and talk to Chef about the menu."

Dover bowed, face serious. "Yes, your highness."

Eugenia gave him a quick hug, then swam away.

Dover looked around the hallway. "Chubber, did that really happen?"

～

BY THE TIME Dover got home, he was exhausted. Being a prince sucked ass.

Rachael clucked at him as he walked past her. "Hey, guard chicken. Keep up the good work."

Shauna met him on the porch with the biggest smile he had ever seen. She hugged him tight, trapping Chubber between them. "Bluetail, I hear you're pregnant."

He hugged her back hard, burying his face in her hair. Goddess, Shauna's hugs were the best. She loved him and always would. His own mother's hateful words echoed in his head and he started to sob.

Chubber squeaked and slid to his shoulder so he could hug Dover's head.

"Oh, Dover. What's wrong?" Shauna stroked his back.

He cried into her hair, letting the pain out. He wouldn't say what the Queen had said. He didn't want to give her words any more life.

"Love, what's wrong?" Ben's strong arms wrapped around him from behind and he pulled Dover, Chubber, and Shauna all into a hug. "Who do I need to kill?"

"Attending court sucks," he finally muttered. "On the plus side, I think Eugenia isn't as horrible as I thought she was."

Shauna felt his forehead. "Dear goddess, you must be sick to say such a thing."

He laughed, tears still falling, then turned into Ben's embrace. "I'll be okay. It's just been a really long day."

Ben winced. "Well, um, I may add to that long day."

Dover tried to give him a stern look. "How much trouble can a house husband/artist/chicken sitter get into?"

Ben pulled him over to the dick shaped water fountain. Swimming inside the shallow water was an adorable baby with fluffy blond hair. His brown tentacle tail contracted and relaxed as he moved.

Ben gave him a worried look. "I kinda adopted a baby today. I named him Shawn because I know how much you love Shauna."

Dover stared at the tentacle tailed baby and started laughing. His cruel monstrous human mate had taken in an innocent that the *kind* merfolk nobles would rather toss into The Deep.

He laughed hard, bending down and bracing his hands on his knees. "Fuck, Ben. I love you so damn much."

CHAPTER 17

a few days later, Ben sat in a wooden chair on the bank of Dover's creek. Otis sprawled at his side and Rachael clucked as she walked around his chair, pecking at the grass.

They had brought Shawn out for a morning swim and found the chair and a gold baby bracelet with light delicate shark-eye shells and small, chocolate pearls. The clasp was a tiny gold octopus.

He ran his fingers over the bracelet and watched Dover and Shawn play in the shallow waters. It was just a little too big for Shawn, but in a few months, it would fit perfectly.

"You're such a smart baby, aren't you?" Dover held Shawn's hands as he swam through the water. "Swimming is much easier than walking isn't it? Oh, look at the pretty turtle. Ben, we're catching this turtle and naming him Henry. We'll need to add onto the fountain."

Shawn giggled as he reached for the turtle, then made a grumpy face as it swam away.

Ben laughed. "Sorry, baby boy. Henry doesn't want to live in the fountain."

Chubber bounded off the rock he'd been sunbathing on and started after the turtle. *Maybe we will need to add on to the fountain.*

Otis' head shot up and Rachael glared toward the driveway.

Ben groaned when a familiar limo pulled into the driveway. "Please tell me we don't have to go to the throne room today."

"I do around lunch, but you have baby duty," Dover said, watching the limo. "We need to fix the driveway, don't we?"

Ben thought of the shocks on his truck. "Yes, we really do."

The driver got out and opened the back door. A stunning blond woman in a flowing golden sundress got out. She wore an elaborate crown, reminding Ben of the mermaid from The Deep.

Four guards also got out of the car, eyes surveying the area for trouble.

"Mother," Dover said, voice trembling. His eyes filled with pain. "What the fuck does she want?"

Ben stood up, growling. Late last night, Dover had finally told him what the woman had said. "I'll find out. You stay with Shawn and find that turtle again."

Dover gave him a thankful smile. "I'll be here if she needs anything from me. I just want her to leave."

"Otis, Rachael, stay," Ben ordered, then walked up

the trail, meeting the Queen halfway. He gave her an awkward bow. "What do you want? Uh, your majesty."

Queen Kelby arched a brow. "I come to visit my son, and this is the greeting I get?"

Ben glared at her. "I held him for most of the night last night as he cried over what you said. What the fuck do you want?"

The guards immediately turned their backs, giving them as much privacy as possible.

The Queen closed her eyes and looked pained. "I need to talk to him."

Ben heard Dover's familiar steps behind him and turned, taking Shawn from his mate. "You don't have to do anything you don't want to, love."

Dover leaned up and kissed his chin. "I know." He turned to the Queen. "Mother?"

Queen Kelby was quiet for a moment. "Guards, wait for me by the car. I need privacy."

They bowed, then walked away.

"I'm surprised your ladies aren't here," Dover said, looking puzzled. "I've never seen you outside of the castle, Mother."

The Queen stepped forward and cupped Dover's cheek. "I said some horrible things, Dover. I need you to understand that I didn't mean them. I can't bear the idea of you thinking I wanted to abandon you as a baby."

Dover's eyes watered and Ben wanted to punch something. "If you didn't mean them, then why did you say them?" Ben asked.

She met his eyes, then looked down. "When I heard

the mating call, so many years ago, I followed it and met my mate. He was another omega and a guppy tail. I fell in love with him, Dover."

"Why marry Father then? Shauna told me you didn't even meet Father in person until the day of the wedding," Dover said, shaking his head.

Queen Kelby gave a broken laugh. "Because I was weak. My parents told me they would disown me and I couldn't stand up to them. Dover, I was so angry with you because *you* did what I should have done. You are so brave, my darling guppy prince."

Dover hugged his mother. "I'm sorry, Mother. I can't imagine living without Ben."

She froze for a moment, then wrapped her arms around him. "My decision started me on a very complicated path and at the time I thought I would die. In a better world, we wouldn't have had to ignore the call out of fear of persecution. I'm truly happy for you, Dover. Even if your mate is human. I suppose he can't help it."

Ben looked over his shoulder. "Otis, Rachael, come!"

His chicken ran as fast as she could, but Otis reached them first, Chubber on his back. Ben's dog sniffed the Queen's skirts, then sat at her feet and waited to be petted. *Damn it.* By the time Rachael got there, Otis had already determined there was no danger, so his chicken turned her back and pecked at the grass.

The Queen smirked at him as if she knew what he

was trying to do. Her eyes fell on Shawn. "I suppose this is the child I've heard so much about?"

"How have you heard about him?" Dover asked, frowning.

"Everyone knows your mate took in a tentacle tail," the Queen said, lips forming a delicate moue. "Expect to be called to the throne room soon."

Ben kissed the baby's soft blond hair. "This is Shawn, our son. He's not just some tentacle tailed stranger."

She watched the boy for a moment in silence. "I'll let you boys get back to your day." She turned and started toward the car. "Eugenia and I are planning the wedding and it *will* take place at the castle. Accept it and move on. Oh, and for the goddess' sake, pave your driveway. It's horrible."

Dover watched her go. "Damn it, I don't want you two to have to attend court."

"We'll do what we need to," Ben said and pulled Dover into a kiss. "Shawn needs a diaper. I'm kinda disappointed he peed down my arm and didn't spray your mother."

Dover laughed hard enough he snorted. "You didn't say anything!"

"You two were having a heart to heart," Ben said wrinkling his nose. "We should keep a storage box down at the creek with diapers and clothes."

Dover cooed. "Come on, baby boy. Let's go get you cleaned up. Are you hungry?"

Shawn chewed his fist and grinned.

"You're starving, aren't you, baby? Daddy will make

it all better," Dover said and pulled Shawn away from Ben. "Your other daddy needs to take a shower. He smells like pee."

After a quick shower and breakfast, Ben sat with Dover and Shawn on the porch and watched Otis and Chubber run from Rachael.

Dover giggled when Rachael jumped on Otis' back and started clucking. He sat up straight and gave Ben a guilty look. "I forgot to show you what Shauna did for me yesterday."

"What did she do?"

Dover smiled shyly. "Come look."

Ben stood up and cuddled Shawn close. He followed Dover up the stairs and past Shawn's nursery to one of the back bedrooms.

"I haven't been in this room yet," Ben said and walked in behind Dover.

"Shauna worked on it while you were helping Eloise stake out where they're going to build the house." Dover had given Eloise and Nami a few acres on the other side of his creek, and Eloise was determined to build their home herself.

Dover waved around the room. "This is your workshop."

"Dover," Ben said, voice cracking. A sturdy wooden worktable sat in front of the windows and shelves lined the walls, filled with all the treasures he had gathered over the last year and many bits and pieces he had never seen before. All his tools were unpacked and ready to use.

In the corner, a playpen was set up for Shawn

alongside a dog bed for Otis. The crown Fergus had left him sat on the top of one of the shelves.

"Thank you, Dover. I need to let Shauna know how much I appreciate this." He rubbed a hand over his springy hair. "It's hard to believe we've been here less than a week. It feels like home."

The ping of a text interrupted them. Dover frowned and looked at his phone. Ben still thought it strange Dover carried one around now. He hadn't brought one with him to South Carolina and he had never kept one on him while they lived at the beach house. Now that he was determined to be a good prince, he carried it everywhere.

Dover swore. "Kai says we've been ordered to Father's throne room. Now. He's sending the limo."

"We'll deal with it, alright?" Ben took his hand and squeezed it. "Should I wear the crown?"

Dover nodded. "Yeah. Let's put Shawn's bracelet on him too. Maybe it will remind them that you two *are* part of the royal family. Damn it, I need to find my own crown. Chubber! Where is it?"

They dressed quickly and Ben packed Shawn's diaper bag. They made it down stairs right when the limo pulled up.

"We could just take my truck," Ben mumbled.

"We don't have a car seat for Shawn," Dover said, gasping. "We're the worse parents ever."

The driver cleared his throat. "Pardon me, your highness. I took the liberty of getting a car seat for your little one."

Dover groaned in relief. "Thank you so much, Leon."

The merman flushed and smiled. "No problem, your highness."

A short drive later, they made it to the castle and Leon helped Ben unstrap Shawn. The merman leaned close. "You have the full support of all the guppy tails, Prince Ben. What you're doing with little Shawn is admirable. It makes all of us wish we would have taken a stand for the innocent long before now."

Ben smiled, but tried to figure out what the man meant. *Taking a stand for the innocent?*

They didn't have time to talk. Six guards hustled them through the castle halls and into the throne room. Today, the Queen had joined them and sat in smaller throne next to King Ren's. Talia stood behind them and looked furious.

The room seemed even fuller than before.

"Ow," Dover said, rubbing his head. "Fucking buzzing."

Ben frowned. "Are you okay, love?"

"There they are," Lord Eades said, voice full of disgust. "They even brought the creature with them."

Several older lords moved to stand around Ben and Dover, and Ben really wished he had asked Eloise or Romeu to come with him.

Ben arched a brow and rubbed Shawn's back. "I *know* you aren't calling our son a creature."

Lord Eades snarled. "You have no respect for our traditions. Your human arrogance is an insult to our kingdom and the royal family whom you are trying to take advantage of."

Ben couldn't help it. He started laughing. "Are you serious? Do you really want to argue that *arrogance* is a human trait?"

He looked at the King, but the man remained emotionless even as the younger lords and ladies started fidgeting in their seats, clearly agitated.

The Queen exchanged a worried look with Talia and gestured for the guards to move closer.

"How is Ben disrespecting our traditions?" Dover asked, voice frustrated.

Lord Eades pointed at Shawn, a look of triumph on his face. "The tentacle tailed mers belong in The Deep. You interfered in our accepted customs and *will* be punished."

"He's a baby," Ben said, shaking his head. "Someone left him alone on a strip of land and he's only five months old at the most. How is this acceptable?"

"He is tentacle tailed," Lord Eades repeated, voice rising.

"He's tentacle tailed," Ben agreed, trying not to shout himself. "Prince Kai is tiger shark tailed. My mate is guppy tailed. Prince Kit is clownfish tailed. I'm black and a human. What the fuck does it matter? It just is. It doesn't mean we're good or bad. It's just part of us. Shawn is just a baby. He eats, sleeps, and pees and poops. His merform is adorable and just part of who he is becoming."

"You don't understand," Lord Eades said.

"Lord Eades, there is no law concerning the tentacle

tailed mers in our kingdom," Talia said. "Traditions and customs *are not laws!*"

The hate in the older mer's eyes sent a shiver down Ben's spine. "You know nothing, princess. Even a generation ago this would be unacceptable behavior. We noble merfolk have standards and this is beyond the pale. It is time someone took a stand to preserve our way of life."

Lord Eades looked around the room. "I call for a motion to banish the human and the tentacle tailed creature from the Southern Silver Isles and to terminate Prince Dover's pregnancy so he does not bring disgrace to his bloodline."

Queen Kelby gasped and the room erupted in noise as the rest of the lords and ladies started to speak. Ben noted the younger lords and ladies looked appalled while the older generation seemed split. Some kept quiet and sank down in their seats while others nodded, pleased with Eades' plan.

Talia held her hands up. "That's enough! What the hell are you thinking, Eades?"

The King watched the room impassively, and the Queen started crying. The crowd just got louder.

"That's too far, Lord Eades," a young man said from the back.

"It's our sacred duty to protect the kingdom," an older man said.

"This is the only way to preserve the royal bloodline," Lady Belinda said, glaring at Dover. "Perhaps we should consider if Prince Dover should be allowed to breed at all."

Several mers pushed in around them and Ben snarled. He handed Shawn to Dover before pushing them behind him. "You stay the fuck away from my mate and child."

Dover's whimper about killed Ben and he suddenly wished he had brought his knife. Shawn started wailing and the voices in the room got louder.

"Guards," Lord Eades yelled, voice full of glee. "Restrain the human."

CHAPTER 18

Dover's head pounded and he could barely hear what was going on. He cuddled Shawn close and tried to hush the baby's crying.

"Guards, restrain the human." Lord Eades' voice cut through the buzzing.

"No," Dover yelled, standing up straight and moving from behind his mate. "You have no right to make such decisions, Eades. You have no right!"

"We are the backbone of this kingdom," an older lord said, standing up. "We have every right."

"You're wrong," Eugenia said, voice shaking as she pushed through the ring of mers surrounding them. "The noble families are part of our kingdom, but only part of it. You will not harm my brother."

"You've gone too far, Eades," Kai said, moving to stand beside Ben. "The guards aren't yours to command." He looked at Lady Belinda. "How can you possibly think you have a right to decide if my brother has children?"

"It is necessary to keep the royal family pure," Lady Belinda said. More ladies and lords gathered behind her. "It is for the good of our people."

Kit pushed through and came to stand with Dover. "You don't know what's best for our kingdom. All you think about is what is best for you."

A younger lady pushed toward the front. "Their highnesses are right."

Lady Belinda growled and smacked the girl. "Diana, sit down."

That one act of violence was enough to ignite the room. The nobles' bickering took a physical turn and Dover covered Shawn's head, hoping the boy wouldn't see the adults fighting.

Kai, Ben, and Kit surrounded Dover, Shawn, and Eugenia, trying to keep them from being pulled into the brawling crowd.

"Enough," Talia yelled, moving from behind the thrones. "I said, enough!"

No one heard her. The guards spread out in the room, trying to end the fighting without resorting to violence themselves. Fergus, his parents' personal servant moved to stand in front of Queen Kelby, protecting her from shards of glass when someone threw a juice glass.

Lord Eades waved his arms in the air. "This is what the human has caused, Princess Talia. He's led our younger generation astray. Look at us fight amongst ourselves. We must move now." He looked to the King. "Your majesty, we have talked about this. Now is the time."

Dover looked around the crowded room of arguing people, then back at his father. King Ren's face was solid stone and the buzzing was back, louder than ever. Dover understood it now. The Sea Witch's curse.

He could see it unfold. His father would order Dover's mate and son sent to The Deep, then order Dover to have a hysterectomy. Talia and the others would stand up against him. They would fight and Talia would win. His father would die and the curse would continue.

"No," he said, shaking his head. "We're better than this. We can fight it together."

The door to the throne room slammed against the wall, and people streamed into the room. Dover recognized Ervin and Owin at the front. They were followed by several guppy tailed castle servants, as well as Nami, Eloise, and Romeu.

The mers surrounding Dover's group were pushed back and the guppy tailed mers set up a ring of protection around them.

A warm hand on his shoulder had him holding back a sob. Shauna kissed his cheek and took Shawn and his diaper bag from Dover and handed him to Joy. "We'll let her get him out of here. He doesn't need to see this. She'll keep him safe with own pups, bluetail."

Dover grabbed Ben's hand. "I don't want Father to die." He knew he didn't make any sense, but he *knew* what would happen.

Ben's eyes were on Fergus. "Love, I think I get it."

"You do?" Dover wiped his eyes.

As the room filled with Dover's friends, the nobility calmed down, looking around in bewilderment.

"Your majesty," Ervin said, bowing. "We will be heard. The guppy tailed merfolk have followed you proudly for many years. You stood up against your own father for our very lives. Now, we are here to stand up *for* you. Please don't take give in to the wishes of the close minded bigots in your court. You've given them so much already."

"What are you talking about?" Lord Eades sniffed. "We honor the King and Queen by guiding their lives and behavior. I suppose a guppy tail wouldn't understand that."

Ervin ignored him. "Prince Dover and Prince Ben are wonderful young men, your majesty, and Lord Eades and his followers will ruin your kingdom. A kingdom you already paid a heavy price for."

King Ren turned cold eyes on Talia. "The curse is unavoidable. This is my kingdom and you, my heir, rebel against the wishes of my advisors. Another generation of the Rees family is betrayed."

"Father," she said and drew her spear, tears in her eyes. "Don't make me do this. The mating call is sacrosanct. Would you truly do something so heinous and sterilize your son because he has a guppy tail?"

Lord Eades settled his hand on the King's shoulder and gave them a satisfied look. "It is for the best, your majesty. The guppy prince has never had the proper decorum that is required from the royal family."

"Your majesty," Ervin said, hand outstretched. "Please don't listen to him."

"He won't compromise," Dover said. The buzzing hurt so much. He leaned into Shauna. He didn't want to see Talia kill their father.

"Fuck, fuck, fuck," Ben said, then bent to kiss Dover's cheek. "Be right back, love."

"Ben," Dover hissed, pushing away from Shauna and following his mate to the base of the throne. "What are you doing?"

A group of lords pushed forward to grab Ben and Dover squeaked.

A loud hiss came from behind them and a large crocodile moved to stand between the lords and the throne, snapping his jaws at the air. A beaver waddled behind him, snarling at the crowd pushing in.

The lords and the rest of the crowd quickly moved back.

"Your majesty," Ben said, nodding. "You know what's happening here, but it doesn't have to. Today doesn't have to be the day that another generation of the Rees family died because of the Sea Witch's curse."

Dover's father looked Ben up and down, face impassive. "I am King of the Southern Silver Isles. This is my duty."

"No, it's not," Ben said, smacking at Dover's hands as he tried to pull him back. "This is you going along with an idiot's plan to take control of your throne. This is you giving the curse its power. If you order this, your children will rebel. Princess Talia will take your throne and Lord Eades will have more ammunition to turn the people against your family."

Lord Eades' face lit up. "Perhaps it is time for a new ruler. A new bloodline would be free of the curse. Our nobility would be free of this undignified behavior."

Fergus moved quickly and punched the man, watching him as he fell. "Don't you dare insult King Ren and his family."

Kai circled Romeu and Eloise and moved close to King Ren, pausing to kick Lord Eades' gut while we struggled to sit up. "Did Eades actually just say what I think he said?"

"Guards," Lord Eades yelled. "Help me!"

Dover wiggled under Ben's arm. He was starting to get where Ben was going here. "You don't have to do this, Father. Do you really want these traditions for your kingdom? Wasn't it you who worked with your own father to reverse the law requiring all tentacle tailed mers to be sent to The Deep?"

"The curse is unavoidable," King Ren said again, voice hard. "It's better that this happens now."

"Father, please," Talia said, voice devastated. "I love you."

The buzzing in Dover's head grew to a crescendo, and he struggled to follow the conversation.

"She wasn't supposed to love you, was she?" Ben asked. The mers in the room pushed closer, quiet and listening. "That's why you're distant and cold. You don't want Talia or any of your other children to love you."

Dover's father's mask cracked. "I didn't want this to be difficult for you, Talia."

The buzzing suddenly decreased and Dover gasped at the lessoning of pain in his head.

"Lord Eades doesn't lead you," Ben said. "You've used his vileness to build to this moment, trying to make it an easy decision for Talia."

"She's ready to rule," King Ren said. "She'll be a wonderful queen."

"Father," Talia said, growling. "I won't kill you. I'll fucking tie you to a chair and make you sit through one of Lorelai's boring ass parties."

"We have so much gossip to share, Father," Lorelai said from behind them. Dover turned and saw all of his siblings on the other side of Romeu. "I'll make you judge our dancing competitions and listen to Lori tell us all about her latest conquest. She's a kinky bitch. You'll hate it, Father."

The buzzing lessoned with each word spoken and Dover fought hysterical laughter. *Is this really happening*?

Ben gave a hoarse laugh. "Fuck, you make me want to cry. You love each and every one of your children, don't you?" He spun around, facing Dover's siblings. "Tell me, how many of you receive mystery gifts?"

Dover looked at them and raised his hand. All twelve of his siblings raised their own.

"King Ren and Queen Kelby are the ones giving them to you. They don't want you to care too deeply for them, but they can't help but love you all."

"Mother," Eugenia said, holding up her wrist to show off a gorgeous bracelet. "You only ever criticize us. Are you and Father really the ones giving us gifts?"

"It doesn't matter," Queen Kelby said, wringing her hands. "The curse will happen. We don't want you all to feel guilty for what you have to do."

"You love us," Dover said, softly, not hearing his own voice over the buzz in his head. "Even me."

King Ren's face filled with pain. "We love every bit of you, Dover. We love all of you."

The buzzing stopped and a few heartbeats of sweet silence soothed Dover's senses.

"Just like you love your mates," Ben said, grinning. "Right, King Ren?"

"Mates," Kit said, "As in more than one?"

Dover's father covered his face with his hands. "Don't do this, human. Lord Eades and the others will use this as leverage."

"Fuck Lord Eades and the ones that follow him," Talia said. "We are the Rees family and we are given the responsibility of ruling this kingdom. We don't have to wipe his dirty ass for him. He can deal with whatever you're hiding."

"You have the support of the guppy tails, your majesty," Ervin said. "We stand with you."

"You have my support, your majesty," one of the younger lords said. Several of the other younger mers nodded with him.

"It isn't appropriate," Queen Kelby murmured, eyes pained. "This isn't wearing the wrong jewelry at a ball. You won't like it."

Dover looked at his mother and father, then finally saw what Ben did. Fergus stood close to the throne, pain and worry in his eyes. Fergus was always with either the King or Queen. Always. He blended into the background in his guppy tailed merform and his servant's uniform.

"Mother, you never told me what happened to your mate," Dover said.

"Mate? What are you talking about?" Kai said, running his hands through his hair. "I'm so confused. Are we fighting or talking? Can I kick Eades again?"

Queen Kelby stood up, projecting her voice. "I will be brave. I will be like my darling guppy prince." She looked at the lords and ladies. "Before I met Ren, I heard the mating call. It led me to Fergus." She waved to the merman standing frozen next to the throne, eyes wide.

"A guppy tail?" Lady Belinda asked, looking horrified. "That's impossible."

"Fergus," Owin said, delight filling his face. "No wonder you didn't let us set you up with our friends."

"He is my mate," Queen Kelby said. "I turned my back on him at my parents' bidding and became betrothed to Ren. When I finally met Ren, I realized I had a problem. Ren was also my mate."

Dover leaned into Ben. "I've never heard of any mer having two mates before."

Lord Eades finally made it to his feet. "This is too much. I call for a motion to exile the whole Rees family from our kingdom. They are a blight to our people."

Yelling and fighting began again.

Kai gripped Lord Eades' arm. "Guards, detain Lord Eades here. He just committed high treason. Again."

King Ren held his hands up and the room went

silent. "Yes, the three of us are truly mates. I had just killed my father and become king. I had no wish for a mate to love me. I knew my own children would be faced with the same pain I felt, so I decided that I would not mate Kelby. We would have children and a loveless marriage. I would keep my distance from my family and do my best to create a kingdom that would be worthy of them."

Dover understood why he would want to do that, but it was a dumb plan. "You couldn't help but love mother, could you? She was your mate."

King Ren laughed and the mers gathered around looked shocked. The King *never* laughed. "Kelby was easy to love. Then Fergus showed up and demanded his mate. Imagine his surprise when he felt the mating call for me too."

Fergus cleared his throat. "It was… unexpected."

"This is disgusting," Lady Belinda said. "Two mates? That's even worse than simply mating a guppy tail. Lord Eades is correct. It's clearly time for a new ruler."

"Shut up, Mother," Lady Diana said, then turned to watch the King and Queen, hearts in her eyes. "It's so romantic."

"The most romantic story ever," Dover agreed, nodding furiously.

"Because of people like you," Queen Kelby said, glaring at Lady Belinda, "We decided we couldn't openly mate our Fergus. We've been forced to hide our relationship for all these years."

"You can love one another openly now," Lady Diana said, sighing happily.

"Nonsense," an older lord said. "The royal family is out of control. No one has *two* mates. This immoral behavior will ruin our kingdom."

"Kai," Talia said, nodding at their brother.

"Gladly," Kai said and moved to punch the lord, waving happily at him as he fell unconscious.

"Such violence," Lady Belinda said. "This is horrible."

"Mother, I will hit you for Prince Kai if you don't hush," Lady Diana said. "Let our King and Queen tell their story."

Queen Kelby smiled at the younger woman. "We've loved one another behind closed doors almost from the moment I married Ren. I've birthed seven of Ren's children."

Ervin grinned. "Fergus, how many children have you had?"

Fergus met Dover's stare, eyes watering. "Six. We always secluded Kelby so it seemed like they were hers."

Dover's breath hitched and he hugged Ben's arm. Fergus was his father.

Kelby, wiped her eyes. "My dutiful ladies have always been most loyal and helpful. When Dover was born, they even started the rumor that one of my ancestors had an affair with a guppy tail so no one would suspect anything."

Dover turned around, staring at the six mermaids that always attended his mother. They watched the Queen, tears in their eyes.

"Well, that explains why you were always given so

much time off," Ervin said, patting Fergus on the back.

Talia took a deep breath. "Okay. I call for a motion to remove our heads from our asses and recognize King Ren, Queen Kelby, and King Fergus."

A resounding *aye* drowned out the older lords and ladies who protested. Queen Kelby pulled Fergus up on the dais between her and King Ren.

Talia nodded. "Motion passed. Now, guards, detain any lord or lady that suggested removing the Rees family from the throne. That is treason and the dumbasses don't even seem to realize it."

The guards whooped and did as they were told. Kai picked up the unconscious lord's body and tossed him over his shoulder. "I'll let him know why he's in a cell when he wakes up."

The crowd cheered for a moment, and Dover leaned up and kissed Ben. "Is this really happening? I'm so sorry you had to deal with this, Ben."

Ben kissed him back, tongue dipping into Dover's mouth before pulling back. "All this drama, love, and this is still better than you meeting my parents."

"Father," Talia said, turning to their parents. "I don't care about a damn curse. I love you and admire you. You're a good king when you're not deferring to Eades, and as long as you do right by our family and our people, I will proudly stand beside you."

Dover sniffed and raised his hand. "Me too, Father."

"Me too," Lorelei said, raising her hand.

"Ditto," Kit said, smiling and raising his hand.

One by one each of Dover's siblings joined in.

"We stand with you, Father," Eugenia said. She looked at Fergus. "I'm yours too, aren't?"

Fergus gasped, then nodded. "Yes. I carried you and gave birth to you, Eugenia. We named you after my grandmother." He looked at Dover. "Dover is my surname."

"Wait," Lorelei said, face twisting in disgust. "I just realized something. You three have group sex, don't you? This is so gross, but now I can't unsee it. Father does you, then he does Mother. Oh, goddess make it stop."

Queen Kelby stomped her foot. "Lorelei, you are in the throne room. How many times do I need to tell you not to discuss sex in public? And would it hurt to wear more than a bikini top and sarong?"

King Ren raised his hands. "I want to make something very clear to you all. Today has changed things. The curse will not hold me back any longer. I have always given my kingdom everything I could, and now I will give that same honesty and devotion to my family. Openly. I'm finished with living for others. Anyone who doesn't like that is more than welcome to leave my kingdom."

The lords and ladies remaining in the court cheered.

"I also want to remind you that I *am* the king of The Southern Silver Isles," King Ren said. "This is a monarchy and though I appreciate your advice and guidance, I rule. It is time we make new traditions, starting with the loyal and hardworking guppy tailed mers in my kingdom.

They make up the largest percentage of our population, yet they have very little representation here. I want you to think of how we can improve this. We'll meet in two days to discuss it. You are all dismissed."

AT THE BOTTOM of The Deep, a large city floated. Eerie lights illuminated the streets, shops, and houses as the tentacle tailed merfolk went about their day.

In the castle at the center of the city, Sea Witch Johanna watched the scene play out in her scrying bowl, her black tentacles fanning out around her. "Marlowe, they've done it. The Southern king finally broke his curse."

Her apprentice blew his bangs out of his eyes. "It's about time. Do you think Sea Witch Adriane thought it would take them so long?"

"I don't think she cared at the time," Johanna said sadly. Her two moray eels swam close, offering comfort. "I don't think she cared how the curse would drain our power either."

"It's becoming harder to keep the gate closed," Marlowe said, rubbing his shoulder. "It nearly opened today. I literally had to hold the gate shut until we renewed the seals."

Johanna watched the Rees family gather together in the throne room, finally speaking to one another and forging the bonds that would hold them together for generations more. *Well, assuming the gate doesn't fall and release the creature into the world. Then, everyone will just die*, she thought.

"We need our full power. We've had far too many close calls." She waved her hand over the bowl and Prince Tack's face appeared. He was leading his shark tailed mers in another excavation of a wreck. "One curse down, two to go."

CHAPTER 19

*B*en put the finishing touches on Owin's anniversary gift for Ervin. It was a picture of the ocean with a herd of hippocampi. Owin's pearls, stones, and shells each had their own place.

A tug on his shorts made him look down. Shell handed him a small, pink stone.

"Thanks, Shell," he said with a grin. "That's just what Ervin's picture needed."

Chubber's mother nodded, then scurried to the playpen, climbing in to check on Shawn. Their son sat up in his pile of blankets and chewed on the soft ear of his stuffed octopus.

"Ben? Are you in your workshop?" Queen Kelby's voice came from the hallway.

"In here," he said, then bent to twist the wire at the edge of a hibiscus at the bottom of the picture. The stone would work perfectly there.

Queen Kelby came in and went straight to Shawn's

playpen. "Are you ready for the beach, my sweet? Grandma will take such good care of you."

"Are you sure you and the guys are alright with watching all the grandkids?" Ben asked, giving her an amused look. "Does Ren even know how to change a diaper?"

She laughed. "No, but he'll figure it out. He's been looking forward to this since you broke him."

Ben winced. "Does he have to call it that?"

Kelby grinned. "Yes. You broke him, Ben, and now he laughs and smiles and cries. The nobles don't know how to handle it."

Ben groaned. "You make it sound like a bad thing."

She leaned up and kissed his cheek. "It's the best thing to ever happen to us. We can love each other openly now and we can grow close to our children and grandchildren. We're so lucky our Dover mated you. Even if you *are* bringing more humans to the isles for your wedding."

"It's just Stewart and his wife," Ben said, laughing. "That's just two more humans."

"Kelby, hurry up," Fergus said, poking his head in the door. "Dover and the demon chicken are leaving the creek now. I don't want to be here when *it* arrives."

Ben smiled fondly. Now that Ben knew Fergus was Dover's father, he could it easily in the shape of the mer's face and the color of his eyes. Even the man's guppy tail looked almost exactly like Dover's. He also had Dover's sweet gullibility.

"Rachael's been sharpening her beak," Ben said,

giving Fergus an apologetic look. "You better run, man."

Fergus yelped and ran for the stairs.

Kelby laughed and picked up Shawn's bag, balancing the baby on her hip. "We'll see you for dinner tonight. Enjoy a few peaceful moments with your friends before the wedding, dear."

"Kelby, you *did* send the invitations, right?"

She gave him a sad look. "Your parents and siblings declined, darling."

He waved his hand. "Not those. I knew they would. Trust me, it's better they don't come. I meant the other ones."

She made a face. "I did, and let me tell you, Ren was not happy. Fergus and I had to work hard to get him to calm down. Ren had to use the scented oils, then the cuffs *and* the paddle. My ass still burns, Ben."

Ben made a face. "Remember when you never wanted to talk to me? Can we go back to that?"

Her laughter lingered after she had left and Ben carefully finished the picture. "There, Shell. Does it look good?"

The otter crawled onto the table and studied the picture. She patted one of the hippocampi, then hopped off the table and ran out the door.

"I guess she thought it was okay," Ben said.

"Ben, your chicken is chasing my dad again," Dover yelled from the stairs. "Father and Pearl are laughing at him."

"She's a guard chicken," he yelled back. "She's just doing her job."

A few minutes later, Dover walked through the door. Ben's mate's slightly rounded belly was on full display since, as usual, he only wore a sarong.

Dover licked the bit of papaya off his finger, then took another bite of his shrimp taco. "Shauna made lunch."

"Already grabbed some while you were swimming." Ben lifted the picture and held it up. "What do you think?"

Dover stuffed the rest of the taco in his mouth and clapped and hummed as he chewed. He swallowed, then gasped for air. "Ervin is going to shit when he sees it. I told you he went crazy for the picture you gave my parents."

The day after Lord Eades and several other lords and ladies were arrested, Ben had made the first overture and gifted King Ren his most elaborate piece, one of the ocean that he had kept over his couch.

The man had seemed very pleased with it and the remaining lords and ladies had oohed and aahed over it. It hadn't taken long for the orders to pour in and now Ben was booked with projects for months.

Ben set the picture in a chair and pulled Dover to him, kissing him and enjoying the press of his omega's body against his own. "Do we have time?"

Dover gave him a dazed look. "I wish. Moore texted me. He saw George's ship enter the bay."

Ben groaned and nibbled on Dover's neck. "I'm happy to see them, but damn it, I want to fuck."

Dover giggled and bit his chin. "We have a few minutes."

194

Dover peeled Ben's shirt off and pressed kisses to his shoulders, then trailed his mouth down his chest. "You always taste so good."

Ben gasped when Dover's teased his nipples, then groaned when his mate's teeth tugged gently on one nub. The sensation sent shivers down his back.

"Dover," he said when his omega slid to his knees and pulled Ben's shorts down to free his dick. He ran his hand through Dover's hair. "We can be late, right?"

Dover wrapped his hands around Ben's dick and tugged, pumping him hard and setting Ben on fire. Dover leaned forward and sucked the tip into his mouth as he continued to stroke Ben.

"I want to be inside you" Ben said, voice hoarse. He pulled Dover to his feet and kissed him, relishing the taste of precum on his lips.

His hands slid down Dover's back and cupped his ass, pulling their hips together before picking him up and setting him on the worktable.

Ben slid the sarong up, and leaned down to suck the tip of Dover's dick. "You taste good too."

Dover squeaked. "Lube's in the drawer."

Ben laughed, then took a moment to find the bottle. He pressed a lubed finger against Dover's pucker, slipping the tip in.

Dover panted and spread his legs wider, so Ben pushed his finger deeper and trailed kisses along his mate's neck. He slid more fingers in, stretching Dover before angling his hips and slowly sinking into him.

They moved together slowly at first, but they fit too well and it felt too good. Ben moved faster and faster until Dover clenched around his dick, coming hard.

Ben groaned and let himself go, filling Dover's his ass.

They panted against each other for a few moments. "Yeah, we're going to be late," Dover said.

Ben started laughing.

"Benny," Eloise yelled from the stairs. "Are you done fucking yet? We're going to be late."

"We get no privacy," Ben mumbled.

Dover poked his side. "She's your best friend."

They straightened their clothes then went downstairs.

Dover went straight to the table for another taco. "This baby wants shrimp!"

Eloise grinned and punched Ben's arm. "Mid-morning nooky, huh? It's my favorite too."

Ben ignored her and scratched Otis' ear. "Hey buddy, did you and Chubber enjoy your swim this morning too?"

"Woof." Otis jumped up and licked his face, making Ben groan. "Chubber's been teaching you bad manners.

Dover gasped around his taco and picked Chubber up from where he sprawled on the couch. "Don't you dare besmirch my Chubber's name."

"You two are ridiculous," Nami said, rolling her eyes. "Eloise will take the truck, I'll ride Ben's motorcycle, and you two take the Vespa. Your friends can ride home in the back of the truck."

Ben eyed Nami. "Why are *you* riding my bike? Is that even safe since you're pregnant?"

"No," Eloise said, shaking her head. "You can sit in the sidecar on the Vespa, Nami. I know you like Ben's motorcycle, but come on."

Nami pouted. "Dover drives like my grandmother. It's not like Velma is any safer than Cherry."

Ben arched a brow. "Cherry? You named my bike?"

Eloise held her hands up. "Fuck it. We're all riding in the truck. You two preggo monsters sit upfront."

Dover stuffed another taco in his mouth. "Don't be rude," he said, mouth full.

Ben went to the porch and grinned when he saw the limo in the driveway. He picked Rachael up, tucking her under one arm. "Leon's here with the limo. No one has to ride in the back of the truck."

Dover cheered and ran down the steps. He looked back over his shoulder. "Rachael can't come, Ben. You can bring Otis."

Ben scowled. "Rachael never gets to go anywhere."

Eloise patted the chicken's head. "She can go in the frying pan."

Ben pulled Rachael away. "You monster."

Thirty minutes later, they finally managed to get to the docks. Ben saw Hester right away. The older witch wore a hot pink dress covered with tropical flowers. A large brimmed sun hat covered her head.

"Hester," Dover yelled and ran for the woman.

She smiled wide and hugged him. "You look good, bluetail. You're finally home, aren't you?"

Dover nodded. "I needed to come home, Hester. You were right. I can't wait for you to meet Shauna and the rest of my friends. My omega dad is looking forward to meeting you too. He says that salve you sent cleared up the burn on his tail. He won't be going near the hot spring in his merform anymore."

Stewart grinned and smacked Ben's back. "You look good too, buddy. Oh wait, it's *your highness* now, right?"

Ben glared at him. "Why did I invite you again?"

"Seriously," Ryan said, pushing past him. "His highness deserves more respect than that, Stewart. You shouldn't have to ask."

Ben groaned and hugged his laughing friends. "You two are horrible."

Hester cackled. "Show us your new home, Benny boy."

CHAPTER 20

A few days later, Ben stood in front of the mirror and tugged at the long strands of pearls around his neck. "Are you sure this looks okay?"

Queen Kelby and Eugenia had decided to go with formal wear for the wedding. The problem was that a mer's idea of formal wear was very different from Ben's. He wore a deep red, ankle length sarong and a shit load of jewelry.

Otis looked perfectly happy in his own jeweled collar. He spun in circles, chasing his tail, as he waited for the wedding to start.

Dover's desire for a small, relaxed wedding at the creek had been overruled quickly. The invitations had been sent to all their allies and friends and the wedding had been set up in the ballroom of the castle.

Hester smacked at his hands. "Quit messing with that or you'll break them. You look good."

Ben bit the inside of his cheek. "Are you sure you don't mind being one of my groomspeople?"

Hester smacked the back of his head, knocking his crown askew. "That's a stupid question. I'm proud as hell to stand with you, boy-o."

She soothed the spot she had hit, then fixed his crown. "I'm proud of you for being there for your mate, Ben. I knew you were integral to breaking King Ren's curse, but I didn't know how it would all go down."

Ben leaned back. "Wait. It's broken?"

"Yep," Hester said, nodding.

The door opened suddenly and Romeu came in, slamming the door shut behind him and leaning against it. "What the fuck did you do, man? Joy just texted me from outside the castle. Two groups of *special* guests just arrived."

Ben grinned. "They came. Sweet."

He grabbed Hester's hand and pulled her from the dressing room and to the entrance of the castle. Otis woofed and followed behind them.

"Please tell me you invited who I think you invited," Hester said, grinning.

A servant stared, dumbfounded at the two mermen standing in the entrance and the ten guards that stood behind them. King Nerio of the Northern Silver Isles looked like an older version of his son. He was covered completely from the neck down, in rich black clothing. A crown of burnished gold, covered in precious stones and dark seashells sat atop his head.

King Ren left Dover's dressing room and paused, glaring at the Northern King. "Nerio."

"Ren," Nerio said, voice just as sharp.

Prince Tack stood beside his father. He looked

between the two kings and smirked. "A pleasure to see you, King Ren. Lady Janine told us just this morning that you have agreed to let me choose which of your wonderful children I'll marry."

Ren scowled. "Yes, but it had best not be Talia. She's my heir. We'll introduce you to all of them today."

"That won't be necessary," Tack said. "Prince Kit is my choice. Lady Janine will contact your assistant, pardon me, I mean your husband, next week to negotiate the arrangements."

The servant next to the door squeaked. "Your majesties, we have another guest."

Ren looked surprised for a moment, then waved Nerio and Tack to the side. "Of course, Meri. Sorry about crowding the doorway."

The servant just squeaked again looking petrified.

The door slammed open and the mermaid Ben had seen from The Deep stepped inside. The woman's white hair was piled high on her head and her crown was in full display. Her black dress hugged her full-figured body and long strands of pearls hung from her neck.

She wiggled her fingers, waving. "Hello there, gentlemen. It's sooo nice to see you in person. We haven't formally met, but I'm Sea Witch Johanna."

The two kings took a panicked step back, but Prince Tack's smile was all shark.

She looked behind her and rolled her eyes. "Don't dawdle, Marlowe. Come meet the kings."

A young merman with pale skin and black hair tugged at the sleeve of his shirt as he walked in the door. "It's too damn bright everywhere. How do these people function with that huge poisonous ball of fire in the sky?"

Johanna pulled the young man forward. "This is Sea Witch Marlowe, my apprentice." She smiled wide and called down the hall. "Thank you, Ben, for inviting us to you special day."

Hester chuckled. "Your father-in-law is going to kill you."

Ben pulled her back inside the dressing room. "I did it for their own good. This curse thing needs to end."

"I agree," Hester said. "There's more at stake than you realize, but this is a very good first step. Now, time to focus on your wedding. Romeu, you have the ring?"

The crocodile shifter wiped his sweaty brow and held it up. "I'll give it to Eloise before she goes down the aisle. I can't believe I'm doing this for you." He tugged at his own strand of beads. "I look ridiculous."

Ben smiled apologetically. "I needed fifteen fucking groomspeople since Dover insisted on having all of his siblings, plus Nami, Shauna, and Ervin as his groomspeople. I only really know half of the poor merfolk that got roped into helping me out. Deal with it."

"Fifteen?" Romeu asked, brow furrowed. "We only have fourteen."

His door opened and Sea Witch Johanna came in, shutting it behind her. "Groomsperson number fifteen is here, Ben, darling. I hope my dress will do. Marlowe and I can't stay for the reception, but we are happy to be here for your big day."

He smiled nervously. "Hey, thanks for coming. You look great."

She smirked. "How's the baby?"

"Shawn's good. He loves his merform because he can move around more, but he'll be walking soon too."

She took a strand of her beads from around her neck and put it over Ben's head. "That's good to hear, darling. Now, introduce me to your witch."

DOVER GROANED. "I can't believe Ben invited the Coalswells and the fucking Sea Witch. I thought he was smart, I swear."

Chubber sat on the counter and chattered and squeaked. *I know, Chubbs,* Dover thought. *Father has to be furious.*

Fergus played peek-a-boo with Shawn on the couch. "Your alpha daddy is too earnest for his own good, baby boy. Yes, he is. We still love him though. Even if he's a human."

Kit bounced Pearl on his hip. "I can't believe I have to marry the Coalswell prince. Are you sure that's what you heard, Lorelai?"

Dover's sister pouted and she patted her hair. "I can't believe he didn't choose me. I'm obviously the most beautiful on the isles."

"Lorelai," Kai said, sharply. "Are you sure he said Kit?"

She rolled her eyes. "Yes. He wants tubby over there."

Kit glared at her. "Watch it, bimbo."

"Children," Talia said, clapping her hands. "Get your shit together. We have a wedding to get through and a reception that's sure to be extra fun."

Nami leaned against him, "Eloise said Ben looks hot."

"Are his shoulders bare?" Dover cupped his cheeks. "Is he wearing the nipple ring I got him? I love those nips."

Nami laughed when his brothers and sisters looked at him in fascination. "Just think, you could have had this weirdness in your life a long time ago."

The door cracked open and Dover's mother slipped in. She paused, eyes softening when she saw him. "Dover, you look beautiful."

He stroked a hand over his sea blue sarong. "Thanks."

She kissed his cheek, then waved to her husband. "Fergus, love, hand me Shawn and come along. We need to keep Ren from murdering King Nerio."

"Uh oh," Fergus said, jumping up and following her.

Ervin looked at his watch. "I do believe it is time. Princess Pearl, are you ready to be a flower girl?"

Pearl giggled and grabbed her bag of flower petals.

"Princess Lorelei, you're first. Go to the ballroom entrance direct Pearl down the aisle. Owin will tell you when to go."

One by one, his groomspeople left the room as Ervin directed them.

Shauna hugged him before she went. "Life looks good, doesn't it, bluetail?"

"So good," he said, laughing. "I love you, Shauna. Thank you for being there for me. For holding me when I cried."

"My pleasure, baby boy." She cupped his face. "I never thought I'd see the day that the King and Queen smiled. Your mate saw what was right under our noses this whole time."

Dover smiled. "He really did. I wouldn't have found him without you, Shauna. You've always had my back."

She kissed his cheek and left.

Ervin was next to hug him. "You've made me so proud, Prince Dover. These last two months, you haven't missed a session at the royal court. You work so hard for us guppy tails."

"You all are worth it," Dover said. "The rest of the nobles are starting to see that. Ervin, thank you, for teaching me to treasure. I don't want to think of how my life would be without that."

"You came to it naturally, bluetail." Ervin kissed his forehead, then left him alone with Nami.

His best friend wiped her eyes and gave him her own hug. "I'm happy for you, dumbass."

He squeezed her tight. "I liked your wedding more." It had been at the creek.

She laughed. "It was all the beer, wasn't it?"

Dover shrugged. Their reception would be pretty tame, especially considering Father would be glaring at King Nerio the whole time.

"Bluetail, I think our future is going to be pretty amazing," Nami said, settling her head on his shoulder.

"Our kids will be best friends and we live right across the creek from one another."

"I love you, Nami."

"Love you too. Let's get you married."

A few minutes later, he followed Nami down the aisle. The sight of the Sea Witch standing next to Otis made Dover groan, but then he saw Ben waiting for him.

His mate looked delicious and Dover could see the gleam of his nipple rings from the door. "I love his nips, Chubber."

His otter chirped and walked with him down the aisle. Ben took his hands and King Ren began the ceremony. To Dover, it was a blur of words and gestures that went by quickly as Dover focused on Ben's eyes and shoulders and cute little nipples.

"I present, Prince Dover and Prince Ben," Dover's father said.

Ben kissed him. "You were staring at my nipples the whole time, love."

CHAPTER 21

TWO MONTHS LATER

*T*he rain beat against the windows of the cottage. Rainy season had finally made its way to The Southern Silver Isles. Quick, heavy rainstorms were now the new normal and

Dover finished his plate of grilled seafood paella and told himself not to lick the plate. He could have seconds.

Nami sat beside him at the table, working on her own plate. His friend's baby bump was just starting to show and her appetite could almost rival his own.

"Then, Prince Tack came by," Ben said, washing dishes.

Dover whipped around to face his mate. "What? Prince Tack came by here?"

Ben nodded. "With like a thousand of your father's guards."

"What did he want?" Dover fought a pout, wishing he hadn't left Ben alone at home while he and Shawn met Kit and Pearl for a playdate.

"He said he was just visiting," Ben said, shrugging. "He saw your waterfall picture and commissioned a piece of his own."

"What did he ask for?" Dover handed Ben his plate and smiled when his mate automatically refilled it for him.

"I'm not telling. It's a wedding gift for Kit." Ben gave Otis a piece of shrimp and Chubber danced on the back of the couch until Ben gave him a piece too.

Dover glared at his human. "Ben, I'm your omega, your mate, and your husband. Tell me what Prince Tack ordered."

Ben smirked. "You'll have to wait, bluetail. It'll be good for you."

Dover gasped and clutched a hand over his heart. "The pain you've caused me will follow us to the end of our days."

Nami rolled her eyes. "You'll forget by tonight."

Barking at their door interrupted them before Dover could come up with a scathing reply. Romeu's voice carried through the heavy wood. "Hey, let us in, man. It's wet out here."

Ben opened the door and frowned at Romeu and Jojo. "Why didn't you just come in?"

Romeu looked over his shoulder, wary. "Your fucking guard chicken doesn't like it when I don't knock."

Ben nodded at Rachel. The chicken sat in her covered house on the porch. "Good girl. I'll make you another tutu, okay?"

Dover snickered. Ben had taken to dressing Rachel

in colorful tutus each morning. It was completely ridiculous, but the chicken seemed to like it.

Jojo barked again and ran to Otis. She licked his nose and started running around the older dog.

Jojo had grown quite a bit. She was still puppyish, but she was starting to grow into her paws. "I'm surprised you brought Jojo," Dover said.

Romeu scratched his dog's ears. "I had to sneak her past the kids. She's supposed to be my dog, damn it, but they keep stealing her to play."

"Don't you mean *dam it?*" Nami asked, chuckling. "*Dam.*"

Romeu gave her an exasperated look. "You and your wife need to watch it with the puns, Nami. Effie made a beaver dam pun yesterday and Joy almost murdered me."

Dover ignored their bickering and smiled when Jojo came and laid her head on his lap. She would have made her witch a wonderful familiar. He bet that witch was regretting rejecting her. The puppy had found a happy home, though, and would be well loved for the rest of her life.

"Want some seafood paella?" Ben asked. "Fergus made it earlier today. Shauna and he take turns making their sweet baby boy lunch."

Dover preened. "They love me."

Nami scowled. "Mom only makes me breakfast, not lunch. She loves you more."

Romeu grabbed a plate. "You two are spoiled."

Nami made a face. "We *could* do that, if we really need to."

"Yeah," Dover said. "We have skills."

He even attended every session of court. He was a mature and capable merman, damn it. "Ben, can I have some more bread too?"

Ben laughed and got him a piece. "You're not making a good case for yourself, bluetail."

Dover sniffed. "We deserve to be spoiled."

"Yes," Nami agreed. She tugged at her purrmaid sweatshirt. "We're growing babies here, Ben. Respect the wonder, asshole."

Romeu sighed. "I did come for a reason, but you all distracted me with food."

The baby monitor on the counter lit up and they could hear Shawn whimpering. "Someone's up from their nap," Ben said. "I'll be right back."

Romeu watched him run up the stairs, then turned back to Nami and Dover. "I'm not waiting. Anyway, my buddy in the guard told me your father finally sentenced Eades and the others."

Dover nodded. "I know. I was there."

Nami threw a shrimp at him and he caught it, popping it in his mouth. "Why didn't you tell me?" She asked.

Dover flushed. "Honestly, I forgot. When I came in the house after the sentencing, Ben was taking off his wet shirt and his nipple rings were calling my name."

Romeu shuddered. "TMI, man. TMI."

Nami grinned. "Eloise got her nipples pierced too. It's so hot."

"Isn't it?" Dover said, excited. "Once they're healed up, you can tug on them with your teeth –"

"Enough," Romeu said. "Back to the sentencing. Please."

Dover shrugged. "Fine, but you're missing out. Anyway, Father had them each investigated and found some disturbing things. Lord Eades and his wife were accepting bribes from several countries to convince Father to sign trade agreements that cheated the kingdom out of money. More importantly, they were working with several others to discredit the royal family. Eades actually thought he would end up king."

"Damn," Nami said. "Joy was right, wasn't she?"

Romeu nodded, eyes hard. His wife had been Lord and Lady Eades' personal servant and had overheard a lot of shit.

"Father, stripped them of their titles and fortune and banished all of them," Dover said. "Talia wanted to execute Eades, but Father decided to be merciful."

Nami grinned. "How merciful was he? No merfolk colony will take them in. They're penniless and alone in a world that will know they committed treason."

"I hope that's the end of it," Romeu said, looking worried. "Eades is a manipulative bastard. Joy says he always has backup plans and I'm worried he'll rally King Ren's economic rivals. There are several countries that would love to get a hold of our resources and pearl farms."

"Kai and Talia are keeping an eye on them," Dover said. "That's all we can do right now."

Ben came down the stairs, a sleepy Shawn in his arms. "This little guy is hungry."

"Benny boy," a voice came from the sink. "Are you there, darling?"

Romeu's eyes grew big and he looked at Dover and Nami.

Ben grinned and moved to look into the dishwater. "Hey, Johanna. How's it going."

Dover jumped up and rushed over to look around Ben's arm. The Sea Witch's face shimmered in the water. *They really need cell phones.*

"As well as can be, darling. I see Shawn and Dover are with you."

"Hi, Queen Johanna," Dover said, waving before he refilled his plate.

"It's Sea Witch, your highness," she said. "I am very much *not* a queen."

"How's Marlowe?" Ben asked.

Johanna tsked. "He's as grumpy and moody, as usual. He did like the gift you left him."

Dover leaned over and kissed Ben's shoulder. His mate had made a glass piece for the younger Sea Witch and left it for him on the strip of island where they had found Shawn.

"Good," Been said, smiling. "You know you two are welcome to visit, right? King Ren gave his permission."

Very reluctantly, Dover thought, hiding his smile.

"We'll be by soon enough," Johanna said with a mysterious smile. "I discovered who Shawn's parents were. Would you like to know?"

Ben shook his head. "They gave up any right they had to him when they left him on the island."

She nodded, looking satisfied. "I thought you might

say that. I called because there's some water sprites that need help. Their queen is injured and lying low in the pool on Shawn's island. I simply don't have time to go to her, but I know how much you care for them, Ben."

Dover's heart melted when his mate nodded eagerly. "What can I do?"

"I need you to come to the surface of The Deep. Marlowe will bring you some potions I made. Give the water sprite queen one of the light blue potions and she'll recover."

"Romeu," Ben yelled.

"I'm right here, man," Romeu said, shaking his head. "No need to yell. We going on the plane?"

"Yeah. My boat will fit in it, right?"

Otis barked, sensing he was about to go on an adventure too.

Romeu nodded. "I'll call Eloise. She can help load *Bendover.*"

"Don't call it that," Ben said, scowling.

Romeu grinned. "Sorry, but Eloise said that it's your couple name. She painted it on your boat, so now it's a thing. Move on already."

Johanna listened to them plan, a satisfied smile on her face.

Dover propped his chin on his hand and eyed the woman. *If Marlowe can swim to the surface with the potions, why can't he give one to the water sprite queen?* He looked at Ben's excited face. His mate would love to help the sprites.

"I'm glad I can count on you," Johanna said. "I'll

speak with you in a few days, darling. Good luck." Her image disappeared.

"Ben, do you get bored at the house all day?" Dover asked. Johanna looked far too satisfied with herself for Dover's peace of mind.

Ben froze, giving Dover a guilty look. "I don't get bored exactly, I just don't feel like I contribute to the kingdom. You're the guppy prince and have responsibilities. I'm just me."

Nami burped. "Dude, you're an artist. Plus, you watch Shawn most of the time. Why do you have to be all overachieving and shit?"

Romeu gave her a dark look. "Don't ruin our quest, Nami. Eloise is on her way. We're off to save the water sprite queen and you can't stop us."

Dover and Nami exchanged an amused look.

Dover patted Ben's cheek. "Have a good time and stay safe. Shawn and I will be here when you get back." He foresaw a lot of quests for Ben and his friends. Johanna would keep his mate busy.

Ben leaned his forehead against Dover's. "Love you, bluetail."

EXCERPT OF THE NOT SO LITTLE MERMAN

I hope you enjoyed the world of The Silver Isles. Book Two is titled *The not so Little Merman* and will follow Prince Tack and Prince Kit's story. Read below for an unedited excerpt from *The not so Little Merman* – book two in The Silver Isles:

"I don't want to live in the Northern Silver Isles," Kit said, banging his head on the table. "I actually like our parents now, and you and Kai are here."

For months now, the Northern King had been in negotiations with Kit's father to create a marriage contract between Kit and Prince Tack.

His brother, Dover, watched him from his spot on the couch, his hands propped up on his large, pregnant belly. "Father won't force you to marry him, Kit. You know that. Talk to him and tell him you're not going to do it. Prince Tack is nice and all, but with the curse, you'll never have a physical relationship."

Dover gave him a sad look and held up his empty bowl.

Kit took his plate and refilled it with clam chowder. "Preggo hunger is a real thing, Dover. I'll take care of you."

When Kit had been pregnant with Pearl, he'd been hungry all the time. He'd always loved food and had the belly to prove it. Pregnancy hadn't exactly helped him lose that extra thirty pound his mother insisted he needed to work on.

Dover started in on the new bowl. His dog, Otis, hovered next to the couch, hoping for a bite. "One of the others will probably step up. Lorelai really wants to be a queen."

His stupid sister didn't even like the prince. She just wanted to be chosen over all their other sisters and brothers.

Kit sighed. "No. Prince Tack told Father he will only marry me. I think it's because I have Pearl. He knows I'm fertile."

Dover swallowed a bite and eyed his brother. "But you can't have sex."

"I'll be artificially inseminated," Kit said, shrugging. Prince Tack's curse ensured he couldn't touch any other living person without causing them unbearable pain. That didn't mean science couldn't work around the curse to make sure Tack's bloodline continued.

"No, I mean you'll never be able to have sex with your husband," Dover said. "What kind of marriage is that?"

Kit gave him a flat look. "Sex is just one aspect of a

relationship, Dover, and it doesn't have to be the most important one. I can deal with that. I'm used to going without."

Honestly, the idea of having someone of his own, sex or no sex, appealed to him. He didn't see Prince Tack agreeing to cuddle up on the couch to watch a movie, though.

"Is it the artificial insemination?" Dover frowned. "It seems so cold."

"No," Kit said, propping his chin on his fist. "It's just one way to get pregnant and I'll admit I like the idea of more babies. Pearl will be a good big sister."

"Then, what is it, Kit?" Dover asked. "This marriage will ease the tension between our kingdoms, and we've all been fully prepared to make a political marriage. If I hadn't heard the mating call, I would have expected it too."

Kit had known he would be married off one day, but after he participated in the heat swarm and got pregnant with Pearl, his mother had given up on marrying him off. Until the fucking Northern prince insisted on marrying him.

"I've heard stories," Kit said, shuddering. "The Northern Silver Isles are supposed to be a horrible, cold place full of unhappy, impoverished people. They're basically pirates, Dover, and I hear King Nerio and Prince Tack horde any treasure they find."

How could Pearl and he possibly be happy in such a place?

Dover tilted his head. "Aren't pirates supposed to be sexy?"

Kit rolled his eyes. "They murder and rape people and have scurvy. Not. Sexy."

Dover laughed. "Okay, good point. I think you're wrong about them, Kit. They seemed nice enough when I met them."

Kit was quiet for a moment. He thought about the negotiations. "Prince Tack agreed to let me stay here until I conceived," he admitted. "I didn't expect that."

He hadn't expected the prince to compromise, period.

"I don't know what to tell you, Kit." Dover handed him his empty bowl. "This is a decision *you* have to make."

OTHER M/M ROMANCE BOOKS BY
C.W. GRAY

The Blue Solace Series – science fiction/fantasy, mpreg

1. The Mercenary's Mate – https://amzn.to/2MAOFEH
2. The General's Mate – https://amzn.to/2G1abRE
3. The Soldier's Mate – https://amzn.to/2S7R6ng
4. The Lieutenant's Mate – https://amzn.to/2THZ47w
5. The Engineer's Mate – https://amzn.to/2HpI4vH
6. The Captain's Mate – https://amzn.to/2knP03W
7. The Rebel's Mate – *Coming Soon*
8. Fire's Mate – *Coming Soon*

The Hobson Hills Omegas – non-shifter, mpreg, omegaverse

1. Falling for the Omega – https://amzn.to/2BgWURV
2. Snow Kisses for My Omega – https://amzn.to/2TdDiol
3. Romancing the Omega – https://amzn.to/2UNENKD
4. Healing the Omega – https://amzn.to/2FNcXrY
5. A Pint for my Omega – https://amzn.to/2XItQf7
6. Unraveling the Omega – https://amzn.to/2xRCnRL
7. The Alpha's Christmas Wish – *Coming December 2019*

Hobson Hills Shorts – short stories from the world of Hobson Hills Omegas

1. The Beta's Love Song – https://amzn.to/2UrRPNN
2. Bennett's Dream – https://amzn.to/2GwSpG3
3. Justin's Journey – https://amzn.to/2DhW1t1
4. Grey's Gift – https://amzn.to/2BcjxXf
5. Hobson Hills Shorts: Volume One – https://amzn.to/2M3oGGZ

Holiday Omegas Shorts – holiday short stories

from the world of The Silver Isles – paranormal, mpreg

1. Cauldron Cake Pops and a Witch's Kiss – https://amzn.to/33wMrhc
2. Sugar Cookies and a Witch's Love – *Coming December, 2019*
3. Candy Hearts and a Witch's Ring – *Coming in February, 2020*

The Silver Isles – paranormal, mermen, mpreg

1. The Guppy Prince
2. The Not so Little Merman – *Coming Soon*
3. The Sea Witch – *Coming Soon*

If you would like to keep up with releases, please like and follow me on Instagram (@c.w._gray) or Facebook (@cwgrayauthor), join C.W. Gray's Reading Nook on Facebook, or visit my website at https://cwgray-author.com.

EXCERPT FROM BOOK ONE, THE BLUE SOLACE

The Mercenary's Mate – Book One in the Blue Solace Series

Silverlight System, Planet Vextonar

"Next up is a real gem, gentle folks!" The auctioneer leered toward the large crowd at the bottom of the stage. He was a Betonize-human hybrid, sharp teeth a glaring white. "This little girl's part Prime and part Lower. Don't see that on Vextonar too often."

The crowd's boisterous laughter and cheering filled the room. Eight people had already been auctioned off, and the day was still young. Leti Ando gritted his teeth and awkwardly shuffled his feet. The bulky cast on his lower leg made him slower than normal, and there were too many strangers here, too much movement. He wanted to be in his rooms, reading the new Old-Earth journal he'd gotten his hands on.

Draif shot him a sympathetic look. Leti's best friend

was no less uncomfortable in the auction house but had insisted on coming with him. "You knew it'd be like this, Master," Draif whispered.

Leti glared at his friend, his black eye and busted lip protesting the expression. "I hate it when you call me that."

Draif gave him a small smile, dark eyes on the stage. "I know. Why do you think I do it?" His smile faded. "It's her, Leti."

Leti startled, stumbling and knocking into some of the men around him. He did his best to ignore the grumbles, his heart beating fast in his chest. Monty slipped from his head to his shoulder, and Draif grabbed his arm to steady him. For such a small, slender man, Draif had a strong and sure grip that came in handy when Leti's clumsiness attacked.

Leti ignored the grumbles around him, eyes locked on the stage. A modestly dressed woman stood tall. She held a whimpering, blanket-wrapped bundle in her arms.

"This little lady is up for sale," the Auctioneer said. "She comes from a Prime daddy and his mistress, a Lower woman. Unnamed infant, but good potential. Mommy's dead and Daddy don't want a Lower brat, so there won't be no contest of ownership once she's bought. We'll start bidding at 250? Can I get 250?"

Leti sighed and closed his eyes. "I can't believe Father is selling his own child. I hate that he deals in slavery at all, but his own daughter?"

"Yeah, well, he didn't seem to like your opinion too much last night when you brought it up." Draif grabbed his hand and squeezed. "Not that he needs much excuse to beat the shit out of you. It was the threat to sell you too that worries me the most."

It wasn't appropriate for a bed-slave to hold his master's hand, but the two of them had never been *appropriate*. Nothing was normal about a Prime citizen who didn't have sex with his bed-slave, little less treat him like a slave, and nothing was normal about a bed-slave who was demisexual and had a scarred face and damn good fighting skills.

Draif had been Leti's best friend since they were both fifteen. Leti's father gave him to his son and told him to dominate the "broken" slave and prove himself a man. The arrogant Prime often told his son that he was so fat and awkward that no one would ever want him, especially with his attention always on his studies and research.

Leti might be a breeder male, able to have children, but his father assured him no one would ever offer for him like they would a daughter. And love? According to his father, no one could ever love him, not even some mixed breed alien. Being a breeder male showed his blood was too diluted to be human enough. There was too much Wello blood in his ancestry. Father always blamed Leti's mother for it, but never to her face. He was an arrogant bully, not stupid.

In his father's mind, a bed-slave would guarantee that Leti would at least be a man in the bedroom. Leti tried not to complain too much, though. Draif had proven to be the best thing that ever happened to him. He was his loyal confidant and best friend from the start and soon became his assistant, body guard, and overall jack-of-all-trades.

Where Leti struggled in anything outside of his books and pets, Draif could seemingly master any skill if he set his mind to it. More importantly, though, Leti loved Draif more than anything in all the galaxies. He was his brother in all but blood. His family.

"620 to the Drall in the corner. Can I get 630, anyone? 630?"

"Is your lawyer bidding?" Draif whispered.

Leti looked at his communicator. "Yes. He'll keep topping whatever's offered. She'll be ours in a few minutes."

"You father won't like that, Leti. What are we going to do? We can't hide her in your rooms until she's eighteen. I guess we could put her in Wobble's stable, but who wants to live with an Old-Earth Llama?" Draif paused and eyed his friend. "Well, except for you."

Leti grinned. "When I get her, you are going to take her to the spaceport. Talk with Dottie. She's going to sneak all of us on a random ship going out of the system. Father would be alerted if we used our passports, so we have to sneak, at least at first. Once we're out of the Silverlight system, I can tear up your contract as well as hers. You'll both be free."

Draif squeezed his hand tight. His eyes left the stage, widened in disbelief. "We're leaving the system?"

Leti snorted. "I've given you several chances to leave over the last ten years, but you wouldn't go."

"I couldn't possibly leave you behind. I love you," he said with no hesitancy. "What about your menagerie?"

Draif looked at the vexal newt happily perched on Leti's shoulder. "Monty here wouldn't be a problem, but you can't possibly expect to sneak all of them onboard a ship and I know you won't leave them." Draif shook his head, dumbfounded. "What about money? How will you survive? I can easily get work, but you're a trained historian. They aren't exactly rolling in credits." He paused, already forming a plan. "I could work and you could stay home and take care of the baby. You'd be good at that. You love. It's your thing, and in the end, that's all it really takes. We can figure out how to feed her and change a diaper."

"1050! Can I get 1100? Anyone? 1100?"

"Dottie assures me it will be fine. She's picked out a Drellian cargo vessel and my pets are heading there as we speak, even Wobble." Leti checked his comm, then continued, "As for money, I've been saving for a long time. Do you really think I spend all the credits Father gives me monthly?"

"He's always complaining that you drain his pocket, but I thought he was just being cheap. All you buy are books on your tablet, presents for me, and things for the pets. I think the most expensive thing you bought was the tablet. It came from the Anchor's Rest System, right? Our system is seriously behind on tech."

Leti nodded. "I don't usually use more than a quarter of the allowance. I've been saving my pay from my publications too. It's certainly not much, but I didn't become a historian to make money. I never thought I'd have to." Leti laughed ruefully. "I'm a privileged Prime, right?"

Draif let go of his hand and smacked his arm. "No self-deprecation allowed! We are who we are, there's no changing that. Especially on this world. It's not like you can change castes and become a Worker. Anyways, the gods know that no one deserves to be related to your father or psycho mother." He smiled sadly and nodded toward Leti's broken ankle. "Their love hurts."

Draif looked worried. "Are you going to pack and bring my things too?"

"Of course! Melinda has already started packing for us."

"Will she alert your father?"

Leti checked his comm again. Things were on track. "No. She's the one who urged me to start saving credits when I was twelve. Once we leave, she's going to go to Rothwell and work with her daughter."

"Good." Draif's couldn't seem to stop smiling. "We're really doing this?"

"1520 to the gentleman at the front! 1600 anyone? 1600? Going once. Going twice. Sold to the gentleman in the blue coat!"

Despite his worry, Leti grinned. "Yes. We're really doing this."

Buy Here: My Book

Falling for the Omega - Book One of Hobson Hills
Omegas series

Carter loaded the last of his tools into his new work
van and shut the door. His first day in his new
profession was off to a good start. He had three clients
to see today and eight spread out during the rest of the
week.

Finally getting his plumbing license had been a
good idea, even if his perfect, wealthy family hated the
idea of him being a plumber.

Hell, they had also hated the idea of him being a
soldier and of him moving out of state when he came
back injured. They pretty much hated every decision
he made.

The crisp fall wind was cold, but the gold, brown,
and red leaves on the trees and ground made the cold
worth dealing with. Autumn in Maine sure wasn't the
same as autumn in Georgia, but so far, he was damn

happy with the move. There was a peace here amongst the trees that he hadn't managed to find anywhere else.

"Hi, Mr. Neighbor!"

A child's voice came from behind him, startling Carter. He spun around, stumbling a bit on his prosthesis, and faced the little girl standing a few feet from his van.

She looked about five or six, with two black braids, caramel skin, and a freckled nose. When she smiled brightly, he saw a small gap between her two front teeth.

A black and gray miniature schnauzer sat at her feet, gaze stern and trained on him.

He looked around and didn't see any adults. His little half acre tract was quite a ways back from the road, nestled between a good-sized apple orchard on one side and a thick forest on the other.

Where the hell had this little girl come from?

"My name's Olive, and I brought you a welcome basket. I made it myself, but Daddy made you one too. He's gonna bring it tonight. I wanted you to get mine first, 'cause it's from me and then we'll be best friends." The little girl paused to take a breath. Her wide brown eyes sparkled and met his straight on, innocent and fearless. "We'll be best friends forever."

She didn't even seem to see the scars along the side of his face. The burn marks had already made two kids cry at the grocery store yesterday. Both times, the parents had been too embarrassed to apologize. They just grabbed their kids and ran.

"Uh, where's your daddy, Olive?" His voice was

deep and cracked, broken by the scarring on his neck. Her adoring stare was starting to freak him out a little. He'd never really been around kids.

"He's at home," she answered and handed him the basket. "See what I brought you? Look, look, look."

"Do you know your phone number? Maybe we could give your daddy a call," Carter said, taking the basket from Olive. He pulled the small hand towel from the top and almost dropped the basket. "Is that a hedgehog?"

"Yep! That's Hodges the hedgehog. He wanted to come visit too. Oh and this is Winston," she said and knelt to pet the small dog.

"Okay, your number?" He tried to keep his gruff voice kind. No sense in scaring the kid.

"Olive! Olive Persephone Wilson! Where are you?" A man's voice called from the orchard, full of panic and desperation.

"Uh oh," Olive said. She hurriedly looked around, then darted behind his van, Winston following her. "That's Daddy." She poked her head out and stared hard. "Tell. Him. Nothing."

She quickly hid again when a young omega rushed out of the orchard. He was her father, had to be. He looked just like her.

Carter suddenly couldn't catch his breath. The man in front of him was simply adorable. He was short and well formed, a little chubby. His black hair fell in curls around his face, and his wide hazel eyes contrasted beautifully with his caramel skin. The same freckles that decorated his daughter's nose, fell across his own.

Where it looked cute on the kid, on her father... Bad thoughts, Carter! Bad thoughts!

"Have you seen a little girl? Black hair? Brown eyes? Miniature schnauzer with her? Maybe a hedgehog?"

Carter stared at the handsome man, mouth gaping, for too long.

The man frowned at him, tilting his head. "Are you alright?" His shy smile revealed the small gap between his front teeth.

Oh fuck, he was so damn perfect. He met Carter's eyes too, didn't even glance at the scars.

"Mister?"

Carter shook his head and did his best to pull himself together. He smiled, as best he could with the scar tissue, and nodded toward the van, holding a finger to his lips, encouraging the man to keep quiet.

Olive's father rolled his eyes and stomped around the van. A squealing Olive ran from her hiding spot and hid behind Carter, hugging him around the waist.

"Mr. Neighbor, save me!" Her giggling told him she wasn't too worried about her father catching her.

"Olive, you scared me to death running off like that." Her father really did look worried. "What have I told you about leaving the house without me?"

"But daddy," she whined. "I wanted to meet Mr. Neighbor. We're best friends now, and I gave him a welcome basket. I was being hospital."

Carter frowned. Hospital?

"Hospitable, baby girl, and it doesn't matter. You are too little to be wandering around by yourself and talking to strangers. No television time this week, and you have to clean out Pooka and Banjo's stalls on Saturday."

Olive gave a big sigh and leaned her forehead into Carter's leg. "Okay, Daddy, but it was worth it. I have a new best friend now."

The man met Carter's stare, a question in his eyes. Carter nodded and gave his best half smile.

"Well, maybe our new neighbor would like to come over for dinner one night? So that we can meet him properly," the man said.

"Yay! Mr. Neighbor, can you come tonight? Daddy's gonna make apple dumplins for dessert."

Carter smiled at the little girl and nodded. "Yeah, if it's okay with your dad."

The man smiled and nodded eagerly. "That would be great. I hardly ever get to cook for anyone but Olive." He gave a flustered look and held out his hand. "Oh, I forgot. My name is Elijah Wilson. I live in the farmhouse with the orchard. Of course, you've met Olive."

Carter shook his hand, touch lingering longer than it should. He was reluctant to release him but finally did. "Yeah, I'm Carter Benson. Just moved here from Georgia."

"Wow, so Maine's probably a bit different, huh?"

"Yeah, but all the colors on the trees? And ya'll actually have snow. I've never seen much of it."

"You say that like snow is a good thing." Elijah shuddered. "Well, welcome to Hobson Hill. I see Olive already gave you a welcome basket."

Carter looked back in it. "There's a hedgehog in

there." His coarse voice was getting rougher as he spoke. He wasn't used to talking so much. Doctors said it was good for him to do though.

"I put cider in there for you. It's in my favorite big girl cup, the one with Moana. There's also butter from Pooka and some of Daddy's bread. It's so yummy!"

"Thanks, Olive. I appreciate it," Carter said. The little girl still hung on his leg, smiling up at him. She was a cute one, he acknowledged, even though she was clearly a little crazy. It was a good crazy though.

"Your alpha won't mind me coming," Carter asked Elijah.

The man winced and lowered his eyes. "I don't have an Alpha, so no, that won't be a problem."

Carter was surprised. Happy, but surprised. This adorable man had to be beating them off with a stick. Of course, some folks thought poorly about single omegas, and some alphas refused to even speak to them. Idiots.

"I guess I'll see you tonight. What time?"

"Oh, is six okay?" Elijah's confidence seemed to bounce back at Carter's question.

"That's fine. I better get to work."

"Yes, of course," Elijah said and pulled Olive off Carter's leg. "Come on, Olive. We better get back to the house. We need to get you to school."

"Okay. Bye, Carter, love you!" The little girl and her dog ran off through the orchard.

"I swear it's exhausting keeping up with her," Elijah sighed. Carter smiled and held the hedgehog out to him. "Thanks," he said, taking Hodges and smiling shyly. "See you tonight. Have a good day at work."

Carter stood frozen as he watched Elijah walk away. He was in trouble. Big, wonderful trouble.

Buy Here: https://amzn.to/2BgWURV

CPSIA information can be obtained
at www.ICGtesting.com
Printed in the USA
LVHW081650070420
652470LV00035B/1844

9 781946 419132